Gain Of Function

By

J.R.Hewing

Acknowledgment

I want to give special thanks to my loving family and friends for all the support they have given me throughout the years and to my grandmother, who invested a significant amount of her time in private lessons and teaching me every night after school. The study program I was on with my grandma gave me the particular time I had with her, teaching me a structured way of learning and studying. The program we were on helped me through life when I needed to get back to basics, and her extreme logic tuned me and trained me for adult life. Grandma would always stop me and ask how I would come up with my many incorrect answers, and she would sit and take the time to explain carefully where I made my error in judgment and thought process. When my answers were correct, she would ask again and build on the positive response. This kind of mental training and creating a logical thought process was part of my after-school studies. We started playing Chess when I was about 7-8 years old. However, I was never really good at the game, but I loved the particular time I had with Grandma. After my nights of studies, I would have dinner, and then my next couple of hours were invested in assisting my dad as he worked on cars as a side hustle in the garage almost every night. My garage work would take a couple of hours, and Dad taught me to do just about everything there was on cars and trucks; at the time, I would rather have been playing baseball or other sports, but that was in the days that as the eldest boy it was expected I suppose. Being exposed to adults and working closely as I did gave me an incredible insight into their thinking and logic. Dad was solid; he would more or less do the same type of training as Grandma, question why I did something a certain way, correct me, or try to reason with me and get me back on track with logic. They invested a lot of time and effort in me, and as life turned out, it was successful. My work ethic was outstanding because of the life training I received as a Lad.

Prologue

This fiction book is about the many viruses humanity has endured and overcome, and it goes into secret labs that experiment with killer viruses and their mutated forms. The characters in the story are from a previous book, and they are pretty involved in the outcome and the final results; this book is also about many different looks at how humanity was created, evolved, and matured with the viruses and unnatural evolution. It goes into what some could see as trustworthy, and many believe is what it is, just a figment of this author's imagination. The story will keep you involved in the journey forward and, sometimes, send you back in time as it reveals the origins of man and how we became who we are today and why.

The author adds twists and turns in the story, and the players involved will catch You entirely off guard. The book takes a turn that no one would or could see coming, and this author will use several biblical passages and quotes that will be explained during the reading or at the end of the book.

The book will open some people's eyes to what is happening daily in the world, and many will question the validity of the facts written. Again, this book is fiction and is part two of the series, with the first book being Doomsday, with many facts mixed in with the story. The Author would like to state that he has no knowledge of any of this story timeline or that the pharmaceutical companies in the world are doing any of the fiction that has been written. I believe they are doing good for humanity in their effort to find cures and vaccines, but one never knows.

At the very beginning of humankind, that period will be measured from the date that Adam and Eve were removed from the Garden of Eden, and that's when humankind's time started.

Some believe humanity's existence started before they were thrown out, but who's right? It's just semantics and should be saved for cocktail parties.

The legend goes that Adam and Eve conceived many. many children while in the Garden of Eden, and the number of offspring varies by different accounts and scholars, so we will go with the numbers that seem most logical,

and realistic, and since Adam's reported age was 930 years, that is a myth because Adam may still be living. If you do the math, you can see that he could have produced well over 500 children, male and female, not counting twins.

It is unknown how long Adam and Eve were in the garden, but while there, they were immortal in lifespan only, and their children were as well; they had the perfect DNA and a blood type called the golden blood today, which is so rare and difficult to find since the departure from the garden and the DNA mix the life expectancy has dropped to what it is today. For thousands of years, humanity has been looking for the proverbial fountain of youth to increase man's lifespan, and that pursuit continues today. Some ask what happened to the Adam and Eve clan after they were all removed from the garden, and that mystery will be put to rest, along with many other questions that have been kept quiet or made taboo.

Hang on. This will test you and make you think differently about the world.

The ending is left open just a bit and may lead to another book; this will take you across the world and crisscross back and forth before the conclusion; please enjoy the book.

Contents

Chapter 1 The Early Days ... 1

Chapter 2 The Year 2022 ... 7

Chapter 3 South America ... 12

Chapter 4 The Rental House ... 16

Chapter 5 The Reunion ... 21

Chapter 6 The Search for the Fountain of Youth ... 25

Chapter 7 The Coded Books ... 29

Chapter 8 Vonni And Nate ... 34

Chapter 9 Mossad And U.S Black Opps ... 35

Chapter 10 Black Ops ... 39

Chapter 11 The Connection ... 44

Chapter 12 Damek Hava ... 49

Chapter 13 Bogata, Columbia ... 54

Chapter 14 SEARCH FOR FILE- BOJ-25:33 ... 59

Chapter 15 The Plane Trip ... 63

Chapter 16 Black Ops Researcher Hanna Torres ... 69

Chapter 17 Professor Shume ... 74

Chapter 18 The Assassination ... 79

Chapter 19 Hanna Torres's Discovery ... 86

Chapter 20 The Jungle 91

Chapter 21 Damek Hava And The File BOJ-25:33 97

Chapter 22 The Mountain Jungle Retreat 102

Chapter 23 Bjoern Connection 107

Chapter 24 The Flash Drive Decoding 112

Chapter 25 BOJ-25:33 File 118

Chapter 26 Asgardians 777 122

Chapter 27 Assembly Of The Infamous File 127

Chapter 28 Gilgamesh and Asgardians 777 131

Chapter 29 The File Room 137

Chapter 30 BOJ-25:33 File And The Need For Speed 142

Chapter 31 Asgardians 777, Secrets 147

Chapter 32 Mission Contact Persons 152

Chapter 33 BOJ-25:33 File Assembly 158

Chapter 34 The Missing Persons Research 165

Chapter 35 The BOJ-25:33 Cure (Two Parts) 170

Chapter 36 Vax Part One Of Two 175

Chapter 37 Part Two, Section Two 180

Chapter 38 The Gignesthai File Of Dameks Memoirs 185

Chapter 39 Chem-Trails In The Sky 193

Epilogue 204

Chapter [illegible]: The Jungle .... [illegible]

Chapter [illegible]: [illegible] And [illegible] .... [illegible]

Chapter [illegible]: The [illegible] Jungle [illegible] .... [illegible]

Chapter [illegible]: [illegible] Connection .... [illegible]

Chapter [illegible]: The [illegible] Decoding .... [illegible]

Chapter [illegible]: [illegible] .... [illegible]

Chapter [illegible]: [illegible] .... [illegible]

Chapter [illegible]: Assembly Of The [illegible] .... [illegible]

Chapter [illegible]: [illegible] Ascension .... [illegible]

Chapter [illegible]: The [illegible] Road .... [illegible]

Chapter [illegible]: [illegible] And The [illegible] .... [illegible]

Chapter [illegible]: [illegible] .... [illegible]

Chapter [illegible]: [illegible] .... [illegible]

Chapter [illegible]: [illegible] .... [illegible]

Chapter [illegible]: [illegible] .... [illegible]

Chapter [illegible]: [illegible] .... [illegible]

Chapter [illegible]: [illegible] .... [illegible]

Chapter [illegible]: [illegible] .... [illegible]

Chapter [illegible]: The [illegible] .... [illegible]

Chapter [illegible]: [illegible] Trails In The [illegible] .... [illegible]

Epilogue .... [illegible]

Chapter 1

The Early Days

Meir Alter grew up in Europe in a section or corner of the Czech, Austria, and German borders. He was born in Passau, which lies near the Danube, Inn, and Liz rivers. Known as the three-river city, it's overlooked by Veste Oberhausen, a 13th-century hilltop fortress that houses a city museum and observation tower. Passau's roots reach back to the Roman Times. The area was settled sometime between 250 and 450 AD and was the Episcopal seat of the Roman Empire in 739 AD. This beautiful town has its old-time feel; the people and residents seem to have stopped in time. They have the same traditions that they have enjoyed for a century. The town is located in the German state of Bavaria. Meir Alter's parents were of the Jewish and Christian faith, his mother Jewish and his father was Christian. His parents didn't practice their individual beliefs. However, the two let Meir choose for himself. They would teach him their religions and explain that whatever choice he made was okay with both of his parents. Meir studied both holy books, and he may have chosen one or the other or neither, but he didn't let his parents know what his thoughts were. Meir's exact date of birth is unknown because most, if not all, of his known ancestors are gone, and the two world wars did not help with record keeping of births. During the Wars, people were coming and going so often that record-keeping was halted for decades.

Meir Alter knew his date of birth and kept it secret for reasons that will be revealed later. He was of German descent. However, the area he grew up in was primarily Christian and Jewish. He grew up knowing both faiths well and didn't believe in either doctrine, but he respected both and could pass as a Jew or a Christian. Meir would use that ability to his advantage throughout his life. When he needed to switch over from one to another, he would change the spelling of his name from Meir to the German equivalent of Mayer or Meyer.

Meir was knowledgeable and could recall almost everything he viewed or read. With his analytical mind, he would stand out above all others. A pharmaceutical company was impressed by his unique intellect at an early age. They kept close watch during his formative years. From the age of 2 forward, Meir was watched and groomed to work on the secret project he would head. This grooming included a small group assigned to his well-being and safety. This Pharma company, Merck, knew he was special when he was very young and decided to nurture and exploit him by sending him to college in 1901 and pushing him toward Biochemistry and research studies. The pharma company has financial ties to the colleges that Merck sponsors. Meir Alter excelled in all areas of Biochemistry. The study is an area of science that researches the processes of life, the prevention and treatment of disease, the genetic environment factors related to health and disease, and other areas that will be named later.

This Big Pharma company, Merck, was founded as an affiliate in January 1891 in the U. S. However, its roots go back to Germany, established in 1668. Pharmacists in those days were called Apothecary. These early druggists meticulously mixed herbs and minerals to cure ailments of their fellow man.

After college, Meir Alter was hired by Merck, a pharmaceutical company, and quickly moved up the management ranks from one department to another. What Meir didn't know was that he was being groomed for a position in the company that was a subsidiary of the mother company. Meir needed to go through the whole management course of the company to understand the inner workings within so he could pick and choose his colleagues for the project he would be assigned. Meir would have cart blanch on the personnel, equipment, and budget for the secret project he would head. Big Pharma companies work under extreme secrecy because of the hundreds of millions of dollars invested in a new drug or cure. In most cases, the projects being worked on are so secret that just a handful of the top executives know what they are, and in rare occasions, just the CEO.

The tens of millions of shareholders aren't concerned; they want their quarterly dividend and the company profitable. In most cases, the research and development are for a breakthrough that may cure a disease, help humanity in other ways, or improve a known drug with fewer side effects. These companies can set up shop anywhere in the world and say they are doing one thing and working on something entirely different.

Many complexes for RSD are set up across the globe; some of the most secretive ones are in Africa or South America, and away from prying eyes, the laws are lenient towards businesses.

Meir Alter would head and supervise several of these Labs and was the youngest executive with this kind of authority. He not only had the respect of the higher-ups, but some feared him, and with that fear, they would try to get as close to Meir as they could. However, he ignored politics and just worked on his project. Meir Alter was the golden boy and untouchable, even to the CEO. The CEO couldn't touch Meir because he was under direct orders from a secret major shareholder. The CEO was on board with this and in full support because, although the CEO didn't know the exact project being worked on, he knew it was essential to this significant shareholder, and that was more than enough for him.

This major shareholder had volumes of books and research about biochemistry from the past hundred or more years, which he would share with Meir when the timing was right. These books' results and secrets are beyond what is usually known in the chemistry and medical world. These hundreds and hundreds of volumes of books have tests and procedures and results from tens of decades of different studies of human experiments, using chemicals and surgery, and a combination of the two; all of these human tests were done in secret and not with the consent of the individuals that were being used as Guinea pigs.

Meir Alter was head of the divisions that researched many different Pharma-type tests, and his most secret and off-the-books research was in bio-research that included blood-borne and blood-type testing. Meir was involved in the infancy part of DNA research. His top-secret research was known only to the company's founders and significant stockholders, and the CEO was not privy to the real inner working or the secret hidden research being performed.

DNA research began in 1869 by a Swiss chemist called Johann Friedrich Miescher. Although his methods were crude and in infancy, they were at a beginning, and the Pharma company at that time was watching and recording all tests performed in as many labs as they could keep track of. This pharma company was backed by a wealthy investor who would always stay out of the limelight but control everything his company did through his purse strings and outright ownership. This man would, in time, put the company on the stock market to generate enormous amounts of working capital and additional cash.

However, he never gave up controlling interest in the company, and his name is Damek Hava. This man had the volume of research studies and reference works that would be turned over to Meir Alter when the time was right. These research collections were not only for the period from the beginning of his pharmaceutical company but also had academic journals of a different kind that were from many, many; most were on parchment paper and in a different language that hadn't been used for a very long time. Meir would have to learn to read this old, forgotten language, which would take time. He was the best one for the job. The time was not right just yet. Damek Hava would have to be convinced that he could trust Meir 100 percent, and that would take several one-on-one meetings between the two, and that's something that happened only on infrequent occasions, and this would be one of them.

Meir Alter truly believed in the secret work he and his company were working on. With a unique mind, he was able to analyze the mountain of new data that was coming in and file it in a way that would be used in the secret project called (HEBE, meaning "youth" or bloom of youth) in Greek. In the books, this project showed that it was blood disorder research for the different types of Leukemia and Hemophilia, sickle cell disease, and others not listed. Because of the projects named, it wasn't uncommon for the many different labs to have test equipment for the research and a lot of blood for testing. When state or federal inspections would be performed, the inspectors couldn't understand the medical jargon being written and were given briefs that were in lay terms and that were good enough for their inspections.

They mainly looked for safety protocols and how the lab's waste was disposed of. There were no other fundamental regulations on what the lab could do experiments on in its secret labs or the not-so-secret labs.

Chapter 2

The Year 2022

There was a horrific auto and truck accident in Chicago, IL Northern Suburbs, on Interstate Highway 94 between Road 60 (east towline rd.) and 176, nestled between Vernon Hills and Libertyville, IL. The collision occurred midday when an 18-wheeler semi-truck was cut off, and the truck driver tried to avoid a collision. He hit his brakes hard and caused his rig to jackknife and turn over. His load was at the maximum weight limit of 80,000 lbs. plus the IDOT Weight Exemption of 10,000, putting the total weight at 90,000 lbs. His load consisted of boxes of metal fasteners of several different kinds, stemming from cases of nails to cases of wood screws and staples. Each box weighed over 50-60 pounds, and the trailer tipped over and landed squarely on top of a Mercedes-Maybach S-Class (one of the higher-end Mercedes, and with all the upgrades and accessories, this vehicle prices out well over 200,000) and is very well built.

The driver of the Mercedes died instantly, per the coroner's report, and the vehicle was destroyed, crushed, as a car may be at a junkyard flattened to about one-third of its original height at the scene of the wreck. Once they were confident that he was indeed deceased, the sense of urgency diminished, and it would take several more hours to extract the driver from the wreckage and more time to identify and contact his family.

The deceased driver was transported to Northshore Evanston Hospital, one of the finest hospitals in the area with world-class Surgeons and the best working teams available. The deceased driver was sent there to be examined and pronounced dead by a certified doctor for records, and a death certificate before the next of kin could be notified; the driver's body was so mangled and destroyed that identification would take dental and other means of identifying, such as his driver's license and vehicle identification and credit cards that survived the accident. An order was given that the family would not be allowed to view the remains because of how gruesome it was. Unknown to anyone was that a person in the hospital administration at the top level gave the order not to do an autopsy or any other examination whatsoever. No blood work and absolutely no other procedures were to be performed on the deceased body. After the next of kin came to the hospital and were informed of the identifying dental X-rays, the body was sent to another morgue for processing.

The deceased man in the crushed Mercedes-Maybach S-Class was none other than Meir Alter. He had just one known next of kin, a grandson named Bjoern Jarvie Alter. He is 36 years old, and he went to Harvard, passed his Law degree, and met and worked with many top law students. He was a brilliant young man. During his early years in school, he came in contact with other equally gifted people, and Bjoern became friends with the most gifted ones. Because the group belonged to debate teams and later a club that would meet several times a month and talk about how to solve whatever crises the world was having at the given time, he also kept in close contact with those not residing in the Chicago land area.

Björn Alter is an outstanding attorney working for the large law firm of Zieren & Sherrard & Duggal. Alter, a named Senior Partner is one of the youngest ever to make it to the position at this Firm. Bjoern was close to his grandfather, mostly because he loved him and was involved in his life and business. However, even though Bjoern thought he knew everything about his grandfather, there was a hidden past that he had no idea existed, and this would soon come to light.

The funeral went as one would expect, with so many friends and business associates from the past and the present, you would think the funeral was for a dignitary or politician. They paid their respects to a closed coffin, and one person who was Alters best and longest friend would not make the funeral. He wouldn't be missed because no one knew he existed or that he was Meir Alters's best friend. His name is Damek Hava, an exceptionally private man who has been out of the public focal point for as long as I can remember. However, he kept a close watch on how everything was proceeding and would intervene if he thought that any of the secret dealings he had with Alter would come to light.

The reading of the will went well with no hitches. Bjoern received everything, including all Alters homes across the country, in New York, California, and several rental properties across Illinois, and millions of dollars. Bjoern would have to take a hands-on inventory of all these holdings, rentals, and land to get a better picture of his new estate, and this would take a lot of time because of where and how the assets were spread across the country. Bjoern was so busy with his law office that he put it off for some time and, at some point, would hire a management group to monitor and administer his holdings and report to him if anything unusual or urgent came up. They would send an itemized bill with costs, spreadsheets, and a summary of his inherited portfolio's condition and future earnings.

Björn would scan the monthly briefing he received from his managing company. He noticed that he had several rental houses in Skokie, and they did well; however, one was empty, and it was a vast house listed as do not rent. Bjoern was surprised and thought he would look into that designation later.

Bjoern carried on with his life as usual for several months, and the interest that Damek Hava had in Bjoern and his business went from intense to casual, and that was sliding to less every day. Damek felt that anything that Meir Alter had that might expose the secret experiments and testing became nonexistent, and Damek could go on with the hidden research that was getting closer to fruition.

However, the loss of Meir Alter would be a setback because he was such a brilliant man, and Damek always had plans B and C in place just in a situation like this. He had groomed others to step in, and these other individuals were as loyal as Meir Alter was and almost as brilliant, Björn Alter received an invitation to a close-knit group he was affiliated with in years past, which most would almost consider a reunion. This group was a group of Harvard and Yale graduates. (I say Yale because Harvard and Yale aren't usually on the best of terms) that are brilliant men and women. This Cabal would meet every two years to catch up and review world issues and politics. Some were liberals, others were conservatives, few were right wing, and the debates would be intense but never violent.

Bjoern usually didn't look forward to these reunions or coalitions because of political discussions and other issues. He worked on facts and looked at everything available before he entered a debate. Because facts can change as time passes, so would Bjoern's outlook or position. Some of his colleagues were not as flexible, and that was when he became irritated because the facts available would dictate the outcome of the debate or difference of opinion. For a logical person; however, for some, they're dedicated to what they believe in; they will twist the facts to make the way they feel fit their needs, and Bjoern thought that was illogical, which was why he would not attend these meetings. But this was different because he received confirmation that one of his lady friends from Harvard was attending, and he hadn't been in contact with her for a long time. Last he heard, she was involved with a man, and they had moved to another country. Almost no one was sure exactly where they were. But he missed talking with his old friend and wanted to meet the man who captured her heart.

Bjoern missed his long debates and conversations with his old friend, whom he called "Vonni" as a nickname, and couldn't wait to meet the new man in her life, whom Vonni calls Nate. S informed Bjoern that Nate and herself were now married, which made Bjoern very happy. He wanted to meet Nate and congratulate him. That time was coming soon in the so-called reunion/conference.

Chapter 3

South Africa

In South Africa, where the first human heart transplant was performed, the patient survived 18 days, and the cause of death was listed as lung infection and or pneumonia. The heart continued to function normally until the patient's death. Some say the death occurred from the natural rejection of the transplanted organ. Given the time and area, or country the surgery took place in, the real cause of death could have been simply the fact that the patient was that sick, as stated, or the organ rejection, or all of the above. In any event, it was a milestone for heart patients as a sort, but the organ rejection was a huge impediment, and much more research was needed. Research is required to determine how the human body would allow a transplant and cease the rejection that the human body's immune system would attack. That was the next hurdle, and many unknowns would have to be overcome. Chemicals and other types of experiments were tried, and the other types that were experimented with in Africa were called "Gain of Function." The researchers looked at different microorganisms and attempted to enhance the biological functions of gene products, possibly altering pathogenesis, transmissibility, or host range. They tried to see precisely how a harmful virus could be made worse. The norm for most animal viruses is that they are contained in animals and don't leap to humans. Still, with a bit of help and coaxing from scientists and researchers and a lot of testing, the nasty mutated animal virus could now, in some cases, transition to humans. Viruses that the animal host may have been immune to would or could kill its human host. These Biolabs doing secret experiments across the Globe are mostly set up in third world countries and countries that are corrupt and look the other way for a bribe.

These experiments have been going on for hundreds of years; however, with new technology and rapid communication, the experiment results could be shared via encrypted internet, and several labs could work on the same experiment using different methods. They could compare the results in an instant.

This would speed up the success rate substantially. These labs and pharmaceutical companies do the tests and experiment under the guise of making new vaccines, and that is true in most cases, but the hidden secret tests that are done are for a far more critical reason. The premise is that they want to make transplants of human organs viable, and the roadblocks the researchers run against are the difference in DNA and, of course, the rejection or attack on the tissue by the immune system.

Again, trying to match blood type and DNA as closely as possible helped immensely, but still, the human body rejected foreign tissue such as transplants. Another method was tried back in the early 1940s.

Before a virus was discovered that would shut down the human immune system called simian immunodeficiency virus, the researchers in their ultimate wisdom tried to manipulate this virus to make the human immune system accept the foreign tissue. The mutated virus was given to primates for testing, and it seemed to work well, but it needed additional work and more testing; the ultimate test would be on humans to see the results. In its weak mutated form, the thought was that this new lab- created virus could be the answer, and a lot of secret testing was happening.

The Aids Virus was said to have been around for centuries, which may be true. Still, the new and improved mutated version developed by overzealous scientists/researchers may have been different. The incubation period for the virus to take its full effect in some cases in a healthy body may take years before it manifests itself or before the patients show any symptoms. During that time, they may have been carriers of the disease or virus and were spreading it. The mutated form proved not to be effective if tissue transplant was allowed. But the testing went on. Researchers in these secret parts of labs knew about the virus and hid documents on how to test for the virus in the blood. Because this virus sometimes took several years to kill a person, and the cause of death was, in most cases, called phenomena or other causes of death, the blood wasn't tested for a virus that was hidden and that almost no one knew existed. It was first discovered or reported in 1981 and defined as acquired immunodeficiency syndrome, or AIDs. However, this virus was around for years, and some would say it was a manufactured or intentionally mutated version of the same type reported in captive monkeys that had the strain called simian or (SAIDS) that causes persistent infections. Usually, these animal viruses didn't cross the species barrier into humans, but that's a big issue, as it's unknown how or when that species barrier was breached. And if it were by typical mutation or laboratory design, some would say the latter. In any event, it was kept secret, and again, some say it was used against some people in the world that the discriminatory ones thought should be eliminated, such as gay men and African American people. There was a conspiracy theory that was circulated for a time that many African children and adults were given the polio vaccine that was grown in the kidneys of certain monkeys and was known to have been tainted with HIV. However, that theory has since been debunked by the

Government.

All this testing and experiments on this particular virus were to coax the human body's immune system to stop the rejection of foreign tissue, as in a transplant. The experiment was deemed a total failure, and the researcher put the study on the back burner and moved on to other ways of helping the human body accept a replacement organ. In 1972, an immunosuppressive-(anti-rejection) drug was discovered that suppressed the immune system and was called Ciclosporin and was effective. It was the start of additional medications allowing other tissue transplants.

Transplants of human organs are a significant medical breakthrough for many. However, the real reason for the study and testing was hidden from the scientists and researchers who worked on the project. It seems that all the money, time, and effort invested would help many, but the hidden reason may never be known—or will it—

Chapter 4

The Rental House

The meeting or reunion was scheduled in about a month, and Bjoern had an incredible amount of work and tasks on his plate, so he had to readjust his appointments and possible court dates to spend as much time with Vonni and Nate when the time came. This was not an easy feat because he tried to set aside five days for their conference as it was called in his calendar, but it was an escape from his grueling schedule and 16–18-hour days at the office that was, as it turned out needed more than he knew.

In the 30-plus days, he had before his retreat, Bjoern was tasked with looking into the one house he inherited and has remained unrented per his grandfather's Will and last testament. A secret amendment or addendum was added to the Will to be read in private and only to Bjoern, and that was completed about 30 days after the death of his grandfather, Meir Alter. This document read that Bjoern would be allowed to enter the mysterious house that was kept off the rental market after one year.

This house was in Skokie, IL. A spacious custom colonial home with about 5,000 square feet of living space, including a 4-car heated garage and fully finished basement, or recreation area sitting on about 5 acres of semi-wooded land that backed up to a prestigious members-only Golf course. The house was maintained till after the death of Meir Alter per the wording of the last will. Because of the constant landscaping workers and general maintenance people, the house looked and had the feel of being inhabited, when in actually it was not; the interior of the home was off limits to almost everyone except for a select few that would supervise any cleaning services that would be performed. The time had come for part two of the appendix of the Will to be read to Bjoern about the house; again, it was in private.

Part of the reading was a video that Bjoern would need to watch that his grandfather recorded, and this video was the first of several that would be available to Bjoern over the next year or when the timing was right.

The video would be a cryptic timeline or history of his work and research, just going over the high points of his career and stating that everything about his life would be revealed in the house. Everything he needed was there, and in the document were detailed instructions on how he should proceed. He wished that Bjoern would use the inheritance and information he would receive for what Meir Alter now believed was correct and the best avenue to go. It seems Meir was no longer on board with his lifelong research —something changed. Was it old age or some hidden information that Meir Alter uncovered that changed his mind and opinion on it?

Bjoern, with the Attorney, made an appointment to inspect the property. Bjoern's Attorneys Group, Grossman-Obermann-Liftka, serving Chicago and Skokie, had the keys and the security passcodes to enter the house. The attorney handling the will was Michael Grossman. He was an old friend and confidant of Bjoern's grandfather. However, Mr. Grossman was not privy to every one of Meir Alter's secrets. Only one person on the planet knew those secrets: Damek Hava, Miers long-time friend and employer. Damek let Meir into or as close to the inner circle of his world as he dared. However, no outsiders entered that realm of secrecy because if that knowledge was exposed, it could and would be catastrophic to Damek and his consortiums, and that must never happen.

Bjoern met with Attorney Michael Grossman at the rental, as it was called, but never was. They proceeded to go through the special security codes and then use the unique three-sided door key that looked like a tee. You had to turn the lock in an inevitable progression of the left, right, and right-left a certain number of times for the lock tumblers to set in perfect alignment to allow the handle to turn. This would also begin the electronic security control station timer, giving you a set time to enter your code. If the code weren't entered an alarm would go off, the local police would be summoned, and other security measures would be deployed, such as informing the attorney of the breach and the Owner, who is now Bjoern, and last but not least, a secret security group of highly trained men and women that were always close and tasked with watching monitors in and around the house. To protect the owner, this squad of elite security personnel was fast, effective, and stealthy, and it was paid for by a trust fund set up by Bjoern's grandfather. This security group was informed of their visit and would stand down but kept themself on high alert, which is where they are whenever someone gets close to the house.

Upon entering the house, after passing the ritual of the safeguards, Bjoern was at a loss as to why this seemingly simple house in the middle of Skokie, IL, would have this kind of security, and he asked the attorney for a reason. Micheal said that his grandfather was a cautious man and that he had reasons unknown to him. They did a walkthrough, and Bjoern was handed the keys. The ring had approximately 12 keys, and all were different. That seemed odd to Bjoern but not primarily to Micheal because he knew Mier Alter very well and understood him as best as anyone could or as best as Mier would let anyone. He just understood that there was a reason for each key and that he didn't need to know. Michael told Bjoern that he didn't know what the keys fit and that Bjoern would have to figure that out himself. After the walk-through, the attorney took leave of Bjoern. Before he left the house, he gave him an envelope to read in private. The attorney stated that the envelope's contents were unknown to him as it was sealed by his grandfather, with instructions to be given to Bjoern in the event of Miers's death. With this part of the will now being executed, the attorney left.

Bjoern began his walkthrough of the residence alone, this time with a more curious and exploring mindset. Bjoern was quizzical about the number of keys that he had on the keyring, which seemed excessive for the house. Bjoern didn't like the mystery, so one of his first goals was to find a fit or lock for every key. There were 12 keys, some oddly shaped, and in a form you might see in a safety deposit box. Others were cylindrical with internal and external teeth that may fit a lock box. He searched the second floor for any doors, windows, or cabinets and found a large cabinet with a peculiar lock. The cabinet was more of an old-fashioned top desk with a locking roll top and locking side drawers. In front of the enormous robust desk was a plush leather-backed crushed velour center and armrests that were so comfortable you could sit at that chair for hours and not get fatigued. Bjoern fished through the keys to see if any would work. He found one and was able to open the roll top. Upon opening it, he found two envelopes, one on top of the other. The first was an off-color, single-textured paper envelope, and the back was waxed. The type you might see from years past when people sealed them with their ring or other classical wax seal minting, with just his first name on the front— Bjoern. Beneath the elegant- looking envelope was a handmade pressed leather journal with a max latch strap. This one was made in Italy. ——————————

Bjoern sat there briefly, just looking at the two envelopes. His mind was racing with wonder and anticipation, and his hands were shaky because this whole experience was entirely out of his norm, and the excitement and mystery were intoxicating. Bjoern began to open the first of the envelopes and read it, and didn't know how to react, so he reread it and gave it some deep thought. He just sat at that beautiful, rich, dark oak roll-top desk in the absolute most comfortable chair he has ever sat in, leaned back, and gave the contents of the letter his full attention and thoughts. Bjoern didn't know how long he sat there, but it was quite a while before he decided to proceed to the large leather envelope.

Bjoern is knowledgeable and quick-minded and can grasp most situations almost immediately, respond accordingly with logic and intellect, and take control. He was never blindsided to the point that he couldn't recover in an instant, until this very moment when he read the contents of the waxed sealed letter from his grandfather. Because of that first letter that threw him completely off his game, he was puzzled, a sensation he had never experienced. The second journal or leather binder put him in a tailspin.

He was unprepared for this and would need a lot of time to digest it.

Chapter 5

The Reunion

Vonni, Nate, and Bjoern finally met up for their long-awaited reunion. Unfortunately, most of the others in their party couldn't attend, or if they could, would only make it one day, whereas Vonni and Nate set aside a whole week or seven days, as did Bjoern. Vonni and Nate stayed at a downtown hotel on the East side of Chicago and at one of the finest hotels called The Drake. They received a suite with a Lake Michigan View and all the amenities one may expect from this luxurious Hilton homeland, boasting about 900 sq feet in the living area. Simply one of the finest lake view hotels Chicago has to offer.

The reunion party was supposed to have 12 people and a mix of both men and women in equal amounts, plus their partners. A total of 24 or more was reserved at The Albert, which offers elegant dining in private spaces for guests and event spaces that provide an outdoor terrace on the third floor and a lounge on the second floor called EMC2, clearly one of the most outstanding locations for any venue. The guests at the reunion all loved the accommodations and the Italian food tables, the entrees were better than expected. This cuisine and banquet hall was a step above the regular time-honored venue and was a setting that these 24 people were accustomed to and expected.

They all reminisced about old times and college days and caught up on everyone's current affairs. As usual, the group would break up or converge into smaller crowds and discuss current world affairs. When Bjoern and Vonni finally had some time to talk, she gave Bjorne her condolence for his grandfather's death and how sorry she was that they couldn't attend the funeral. They hugged, and that's when Bjorn asked about their plans for tomorrow. Vonni said she and Nate would like to spend time with Bjoern, so they set a time to sleep in the next day in the late morning. Bjoern said he had something interesting he wanted to show her. They ended the conversation then, joined the rest of the group, drank wine, and ate at the Italian food table. They had one of the best times that they all could remember.

The next day, when Vonni and Nate met up with Bjorne, they went to brunch and planned a day for the many beautiful sites Chicago offers. The different Museums and art galleries. They made reservations for a late dinner, and the day went uneventfully, but all three enjoyed it. Later that night, at dinner, they talked about their lives in general and how they all moved in the direction they had planned. Bjoern asked Nate what he does, and Nate said he was doing missionary work and helping poor people and ministering to them, and that Vonni was working as a legal Beagal in their country, also helping the poor who couldn't afford the same kind of expert legal representation that Bjoern provides, and they all laughed at that.

Vonni again gave her condolences to Bjoern for his grandfather's death, and he said that he was almost over it until he received the last Codicil to the Will. That threw him in the loop, and Bjoern said he wanted to talk about the Addendum and show Vonni the disturbing private file he received from his grandfather. He said that he read the long file several times, and each time, he was in disbelief or shocked at the document's authenticity. He also said he would like Vonni to read it as a second opinion. She agreed and said she would set aside some time before returning home. Nate said that while you two were reviewing the document, he would visit some of the grand Catholic churches in Chicago. This was Nate's first time in this grand city, and he wanted to explore it independently.

Vonni and Bjoern finally finished examining and reading the file left for Bjoern. Vonni read it, and she was startled and confused by its contents, primarily because of the cryptic nature of the readings and the pages and pages of it that were in code that Vonni recognized but couldn't read. The file was very thick, and most were written in shorthand in the past. Vonni was very much aware of this technique. However, this particular version was foreign to her. There are three known types in the U.S. -Gregg, Pitman, Teeline, and others in Europe. She tried to decipher the writings but to no avail, which bothered her. Vonni didn't like to fail, so they took a photo of one paragraph with Bjoerns permission. She said she would get back to him when she had an answer. Vonni loves and, in essence, lives for a mystery and research. She has always been a bulldog-type individual when it comes to investigations. She would clamp/bite down and never let go until she reached the bottom of the mystery or the truth. That's how she's wired, and everybody who knows her will attest to that. This riddle may take some time, but she is up for the task, and to be honest, she welcomes the challenge. Vonni has been unhappy and has not pushed herself or her skills in a long time. Although she loves her work, she knows her true calling and feels she could do better work. Little did she know, this may be just the thing that would spark her into the natural calling she put behind her some years ago and that she regrets a little, but it has been growing momentum in her desire to do more as the years go by. Like a tiny weed that grows and grows, and you can't control it, or what some would say was on their bucket list, it would gnaw at you until you acted on it.

Vonni would have to let Nate know that she would research this mystery code-writing, and she was sure he would be okay with it.

Vonni, Nate, and Bjoern needed their week off, and Vonni assured Bjoern that she would continue to work on the code when she returned home and update him on any progress. They departed and left for home; Vonni was thinking about this code or shorthand writing the whole time. She felt that it may be something simple and would figure it out quickly. In any event, her research juices were flowing, and she was starting to get the excitement back that she had lost years ago, and she liked that. Nate could see the difference, and he was getting excited for her as if she was getting a new lease on life and hoping to capture the past again.

Chapter 6

The Search for the Fountain of Youth

For as far back as humanity, homo-sapiens have mutated from the species Neanderthals. Some believe they are distinct species because of the limitations of the biological species and concepts. So, for the Neanderthals to make the leap or mutate in the way they seem to have, the belief is that they had some help, which seems logical.

After the leap, the mutated Homo sapiens started to make significant advancements in almost all areas, whereas the species were stagnant before. The new species, called man, would go on to acquire mathematics, make their language, and start to write and do artwork. A man was journeying to become civilized and form their first authentic villages with leaders and rules. As far back as the very beginning, humanity, with their logic just forming, knew that they would get old and die. They looked for a reason why, and in their primitive ways, they tried to make potions or other remedies to stop the process. They had their medicine men/women make the elixirs they thought would work, but to no avail, and the hunt or search began and has never stopped.

Many pharmaceutical companies are still pursuing the fountain of youth. They have developed many products that they claim to slow the process down, like creams, pills, and diets. Most are very good for you, and some will improve how you look and feel, but the results are that your days may be numbered, and your genetics determine that. Other factors will influence your expiration date. Like what harm you do to your body with drugs, chemicals, and pollutants, and some different factors you expose your body to, is the time you have. Bottom line, take care of yourself and hope for the best health.

DNA found in all humans may be the key to the aging process, and much research has been done into this. Some have been happening for over 100 years, mostly in secret. The DNA found in all homosapiens is virtually 99 % identical. It's that 1% that is the issue and what makes us all different and the same in so many ways.

The homosapiens DNA has been tracked back to the Neanderthals. That is where the leap or mutation began. There is a mountain of theories about how or why the sudden leap happened at or about that period, and what experts claim was 120,000 years ago, give or take 30,000 years. (I love the accuracy of the experts), the accurate timeline may have been closer to 20,000 years ago. However, the real reason was the influx of new genetic material to develop a Neanderthal species from what some would call monkeys or primates. This new DNA would excel this primate species into the beginning of the homo erectus and then later into the homosapien that we have today.

The new or additional DNA that was introduced was planned by advanced people who lived on Earth for centuries, or possibly thousands of years before this introduction of DNA into the primates; these people lived in solitude and kept to themselves on their land that was isolated from the rest of the world. The only way to visit this land or country of theirs was by boat. At the time of the Neanderthals, this species didn't have that technology and was considered the Stone Age. Just staying alive and feeding themselves was a challenge. This other tribe or people that had been around for several millennia were quite advanced, and their population was getting larger and larger. They were intellectuals and, for the most part, did not do manual labor. However, some of the population was suited for working with their hands. This small portion of the growing tribe was tired of being the workers and wanted the same freedom and lifestyle that the rest of the population enjoyed. That's when the decision was made to introduce DNA into the primates that roamed the rest of earth at the time to grow a workforce that would serve them, enslaved people, maybe. These ancient people or tribes had lived on a land mass similar to Australia; it was an island located in the sweet zone of planet Earth, known for growing fruits and vegetation, and had an abundance of animal life that this tribe would consume. This so-called sweet zone was like the Amazon Jungle but so much better; the tribe on this land mass would live in peace and harmony. They had a hierarchy of authority and lived by all the rules that were set forth by the original leaders who had been in charge since the beginning of this advanced civilization. Their life span was ageless, and for the most part, they never counted the years because it wasn't necessary. This tribe seemed to have the gift of immortality.

This land was initially located near the equator, and over the years, the Earth's tectonic plates shifted, and their paradise moved to the north and inched its way out of the sweet zone. The paradise they had was not quite the same. The number of people that inhabited this land had peaked at 144,000. Given the size of the land mass, that wasn't overpopulated in the least.

The leader of this land had to decide to relocate to another area close to what they were accustomed to or adapt to this slow-changing environment. They had plenty of time to choose and searched for a suitable living area. They sent their ships out for the search. If they relocated, they would have to contend with the lifeforms that inhabited the new location, and this tribe wasn't prepared for war or warfare because they were intellectuals and never had to defend the land they lived on.

The search for new ground and this unique concept of war or confrontation would challenge the leaders, mostly because this was not in their nature, and they would have to learn. With their superior intellect, they could make high-tech weapons for the time.

Chapter 7
The Coded Books

Bjoern had some extra time on his hands, which was rare, and he returned to the rental house with the unique folder he received from the Attorney. He reread the large files and again was in disbelief at its instructions and written story. He was intrigued by the part of the file in Code or Shorthand writing that he knew about but couldn't read. He decided to take a crash course in reading and writing shorthand. Plus, he would continue with the instructions to explore the rest of the rental house and try to open every door he could with the 12 keys given to him. He found hidden doors in walls made to look like part of the wall. Once the correct key was inserted, the wall/door would open, and inside Bjoern would find another large hidden room that was beneath ground level and would not appear on any floor plans.

These secret rooms were massive and full of numbered books, with titles and codes printed on the binders. Each time Bjoern found and opened another hidden room, there would be a mountain of documents and books, each written in shorthand.

The beauty or curse of shorthand is that there are different styles. Some date back a hundred years; on top of that, if the shorthand is written in German, English, or another language, the time it would take to decipher each book would take years, if not decades. Once completed, what would you have? That's an unknown, maybe a recipe for delicious chocolate cake.

In any event, this task would be more than Bjoern would want to take on, and he had no desire to do so.

Björn would, at this time, lock the doors or vaults, cover the hidden keyholes with the wall pictures, and decide what he would do with all this data and books. First, he would need to decipher the file he received with the coded shorthand, and at that point, he would decide.

Björn would not return to the rental again for a couple of weeks. During that time, Damek Hava's people were watching him, under orders. Because Damek had a vested interest in the information in some of the books in the hidden rooms, and the existence of the rooms was not known to him, he was sure that the books he wanted were someplace. However, Damek Hava had no idea how much information was stored in the rooms. He thought it was a lot, but not in the magnitude and volume of thumb drives. If Damek had any inkling that this much of his personal information was available, he would have been more aggressive with his quest to capture it and stop the massive amount of research, data, and history from ever going public. And that would be so damaging to Damek Hava and his people if the breach of the secret information (that no one other than Meir Alter has seen and read) became public and may completely change the world's view of history on so many fronts, that there may be chaos across the globe. Damek would not allow that to happen.

Bjoern finally returned to his grandfather's rental house to examine the extensive library of books. In the last couple of weeks, he studied the art of short hand writing, sat down, and tried to read the first book listed in the catalog. Since there are several different forms of shorthand, such as Gregg, Isaac Pitman, Graham, Munson, Lindley, Perrin, and Cross (Eclectic), these could be written in many languages.

Because of that fact, the per se coded writing would be difficult for a layperson to read or unravel and decipher in a logical form.

The original file that Bjoern received from his grandfather had a peculiar paragraph or line near the bottom of the first page, and the wording didn't make sense to Bjoern, who saw it as just a riddle at best, ạ Ω̣ +, - 1111+(0,1,1,2,3,5,8,13,21,34,55,89,144,233) #+-%~*

This particular code or equation would come up throughout the mountain of manuscripts and written shorthand documents in the hidden storage rooms, which may be the key to the secret meaning of the mysterious writings.

Damek Hava had no idea that Meir Alter had these documents and thought that Meir had only a handful of folders, and the folders that Damek was interested in were what Meir had been working on for the last fifty years. The previous communication between Damek and Meir was that Meir had made a breakthrough in the experiments. He had final favorable results, with all the data, formulas, tests, and procedures to make the project infallible. This solution to the project that has been worked on by so many great scientists over the years, with countless hours and hours of work, would come to fruition.

Damek wanted this final set of documents more than he could express. The end product was so close and yet just out of reach, all because of a freak accident that killed Meir Alter.

Damek would now put on a team of investigators to search and locate the missing files. These highly secret teams of researchers or detectives have worked for Damek before, and this "Dark Secret crew" is called the Order of the Knights of Noah. They would be thorough, leave no stone unturned, and do whatever needed to be done to achieve their task or assignment, which means whatever it takes. This group or company has been around for over a hundred years and is used by Kings and High-Ranking Dignitary across the world to locate and uncover whatever task was given to them; this group is so secretive that only a select few people know of their existence, and less actually know how to contact them. Then there is the problem if this secret group were to take your case, and only if you have worked with them before or have impeccable references. The costs involved are off the charts. They worked so quietly and behind the scenes that they are almost undetectable by almost every international intelligence group, save the Mossad, as they keep a close eye on this group and have a mole that works in secret within them.

The Mossad keeps a file of all the assignments that the Noah group works on, and most of the time, even the great agency "Mossad" can't get the identity of the originator of the assignment. That secret was kept close, and just three of the top overseers and no one else would know. Sometimes, Mossad would figure out when the project was completed simply by eliminating who's who, what was being investigated, and the results. But that would take time, and time, in most cases, was of the essence.

The Mossad has a file on Meir Alter, and they may be the only intelligent gathering group with it. Mostly because Meir was kept under the radar, but his constant travels worldwide and most of his trips to Africa caught Mossad's attention. But just for observation, at first, he was a person of interest, and later, he became more attractive, which would cause Mossad to bring his name up the ladder of people of interest to them. They hacked his computer and found so many documents coded in a way that even their best computer forensics and decoders couldn't break. However, the

Mossad had a copy of whatever they could hack into their database. Under the seemingly unbreakable encryption code, they knew that Meir was someone they needed to monitor and keep tabs on. They didn't understand what Meir Alter was into, but the Mossad didn't like mysteries. They dealt with facts and knew he worked for a big pharmaceutical company, but not what he was working on. Again, this didn't fare well with them, so his name went much higher on their watch list.

Chapter 8

Vonni And Nate

Vonni and Nate made it home to South America without incident, and they returned to their work, Nate as a Missionary and Vonni as an Attorney at law for the poor and oppressed. They got back to their routine. When Vonni looked at her phone's photos and retrieved the ones she took from Bjoern's folder that was seemingly done in shorthand, she printed them out and placed them on her desk for a future project. She always liked puzzles or mysteries, and since she could read and write essential shorthand, she thought this would be easy, and she would work on it when she had time. However, it bothered her that even her basic knowledge in shorthand was lacking when it came to what she printed out, so the seeds of intrigue and captivation would pull her back to the printed photos, in a way, close to the meaning, curiosity killed the cat. Vonni's thirst for knowledge would bring her back to the printed pictures of the shorthand writings sooner rather than later, and in one of the photos, she had the bottom of the printing with the code that seemed benign. However, Vonni never took anything at face value. She would invest additional time on the coder equation ạ Ω̣ +, - 1111+ (0,1,1,2,3,5,8,13,21,34,55,89,144,233) #+-%~* and run it through her computer for fun.

Chapter 9

Mossad And U.S Black Opps

The Mossad has always been ahead of most of the world in Secret Intelligence, as good in most areas and better in some as the United States. Between the two agencies, they are by far the best in the world, with the U.K. in the mix. The Mossad has some files that have been going back for a very long time, and one of the files just went Red. When that occurs, the file would go through a complete R and D, and several agents would pour over the data from the beginning to the end and make sure that the subject matter should indeed go Red. This may take some time, depending on the size of the files and how much additional research the agents would need to do. After the research and development of the said new Red file, the group would make a brief and in the brief, which may be a hundred pages long or more, they would break down why the file is Red, why it should stay red, and if the file needs to be reevaluated. If the file was downgraded to a different setting than Red, they would need to have a brief written. Time is always of the essence when it comes to the Mossad, and they will work as many hours on this new Red file and as quickly and accurately as possible as needed.

The file that went Red had data and intel on labs across the world, what these labs were working on, and more importantly what the secret sections were working on. The Mossad had sub-files on every known hidden black lab research project going on and they thought that some if not most of these labs were working together. But again big Pharma had its way of concealment and encryption and everything else to stay under the radar, and out of the Media with no trails or breadcrumbs to follow.

The United States Black Ops file also went Red, and they did the same thing. This Company didn't like surprises so they would go over everything they had, and this group may have more than the Mossad in some areas and less in others, but the mere fact that the file went red at the same time as the Israelis should tell you that they are close to the same quality of intel experts.

An Israeli college professor was having lunch with an old friend of his Elija Lior, they were old colleagues who had worked in the same field a long time ago. The professor, whom everyone on campus referred to as Professor Schume, (the name was shortened because that's what college kids did with their professors' names, and the professor was okay with the abbreviated form), he and his old friend decided a long time ago, not to talk shop. Some because they both agreed in part, on almost everything but they didn't always agree on how to go about solving the problems at hand. So they usually just talked about politics and the state of the union, and how well Israel was doing, and what they thought should be changed, and the two men loved the debate. Elija Lior always ended up giving up some secret that he knew during the debates, and with the secret information he had, he hoped winning the debate would lean toward him. Some of the secret cases were already known by the professor, and this would inferiorate Elija Lior, because the intel was supposed to be kept top secret and it irritated him that the professor had it at all.

Elija Lior was a Mossad and a secret agent that only the professor knew of Elija's profession. After some time, they would finally get into discussing the newly formed Red file and Elija would state that they were doing the research and trying to ascertain if the file should go Red. The professor said that from what he has heard he thinks that it is a high probability and that he has some personal knowledge of the contents of the Red file. Elija understood exactly what the professor meant.

The red file would now be on the desk of a top agent to review and consider what to do next. That it would be above his pay grade and that this file had some very interesting information. The agent that was reviewing this new Red file, was wondering why it went Red after the person of interest just passed away. That was unusual in itself, and again the file in hand is just the briefed portion of the whole file so this agent didn't have the full picture. The file that went Red was on Meir Alter.

The Mossad was aware of Mier's occupation, and involvement in the Pharmaceutical companies and kept tabs on whom he spoke with and or went to social functions, they had a complete dossier on as much of Mier's life as they could get, however, some of the people he met, the Mossad didn't have identities to, and that always bothers them. The file that this agent had, went into details about what Mier Alter was working on, at least what they think he was into, and the file shows that he was working on genetics, blood types, stem cells research, and splicing of the genes, he was also looking at different types of viral submicroscopic agents. The main project that Mier was working on for years was coined —BOJ-25:33— and the file name didn't have any meaning to the agents or most that would read it, the file number just looked like what it was supposed to look like, a common file related number. Not like anything that the government puts on their files or missions with specific code names that would give a general idea of what the mission or file is about. Mier always played with numbers so it would make everything enshrouded, and obscure. This file was no different, the file number could be decoded by the secret management solution that has the master key to decoding his works, and without it the writing would not always make sense or they may be inaccurate. Mier has been around for many, many years and he was by far incomparably the most brilliant mathematician and intellectual of the 19th and 20th centuries bar none. Even Hawkins was a distant second to Mier Alter, however, it was never disclosed or published because Mier was hired and paid large sums of money to do the work he wanted and liked. Plus he was required to work on a special top-secret project. His intellect was kept secret from the world by his employer and best friend, Damek Hava, and this arrangement would work well for both men. Mier Alter was by far the most brilliant human on Earth, and with his total recall and photographic memory, mixed in with his superior mathematic ability, he was exactly what Damek was looking for to help with the research, and to isolate the remedy for the project that Damek has been occupied with for as far back as he wished to remember. Damek Hava is a secret shareholder in many Pharma companies, and if anyone tried to locate or research Damek Hava they would come up empty because this man was a master at staying completely sequestered and almost seclusive from prying eyes. No one knows how old Damek is or his history, and he has never shown up on any watch list by the Mossad or other intel groups. As far as the world knew this man never existed, and here he was in full life with riches beyond comparison and he would travel as an unidentified person.

Chapter 10

Black Ops

The United States Black Ops went over the new Red file and found some information that alarmed them. They would need to do more research to prove or disprove the data they had. At the same time, the Mossad was going through the same motions, and at some point, the two agencies would lock horns or cross paths in their investigations. Conflicts would almost always occur between intel agencies. That's when the two or more companies involved would need a liaison or emissary to bridge the gap. These two high-level/low-profile agencies would then have a specialty group that has worked well in the past that the two secret intelligence groups would agree on. However, that's down the road if needed and would be used only if necessary.

The file went Red because of the inside moles/spies that are in the secret part of the many labs around the world. The information they presented individually was not damming, but when the secret files from each lab were gathered and assembled they spelled a different story. Then the connection, or putting it all together was done by an overzealous, overqualified researcher Hanna Torres. She would happen to see a connection that no one else saw. She would then ask her superior if she could pursue her suspicion and was given the leeway. Hanna worked for the United States Black OPs division and that whole department is so secretive that just a few top people in Washington know what they are assigned to. Hanna started to assemble the mountain of files that were uploaded to the agency in a way that unless you didn't have a background in bioscience, chemicals, or pharmaceuticals, the connections in the files wouldn't have been made. Hanna had a bachelor's degree in biologics and she felt the connection rather than saw it, the feeling was that all of the Labs were working on a project that was in different phases of the experiments, in it was that one lab would use a formula or technique that had minor differences to it and they would monitor each test and record the results. The secret labs tested the use of stem cell research, DNA splicing, and blood work. They had a section that worked on viruses, and they tried to see if one blood type would react differently than another and or if one DNA had a different outcome.

Hanna Torres had been working on the lab files for about two years and had put together her personal file on it. Hanna's research showed that these Secret labs purchased and experimented on aborted babies and their stem cells. They worked on these DNA samples for a hidden goal that Hanna still didn't know what the end game was, but she didn't like where the testing was headed. Hanna had access to every secret file that was uploaded from the secret labs and on a hunch she tried to search who owned these labs. The results were that they always came back to the many big pharma and some smaller companies that owned them, or some that were controlled by shell companies. Seems some of the testings were for what is called Virophages, and in this research, these viruses infect and weaken other viruses and cripple the other replicating ability. The bad virus will then die on its own momentum.

Hanna put the files in order in a way that made sense to her and she saw something that she thought was odd and put it aside for another look at a later date, or when she completed the file building. That would mean, all of the available files that she had.

This would take time and a lot of computer space and she had a program that would help her organize the files to her specifications, Hanna was excited by what she thought she found hidden in the research projects the labs were running, and these individual labs did not know what the end game was Each lab was working on a specific set of goals and projects. Another lab was working on part two, and another part three. Each lab's experiments by themselves are important but they couldn't, and didn't see the big picture or the end product. They were set up that way in an effort to hide the secrets that were right in front of them, like a giant jigsaw puzzle that was laid upside down and you can't see the graphics, but all the pieces are there.

Some labs were working on the origin of viruses, in general, tracing the mutation back. They found to date that a clear explanation for the origin of viruses exists. Scientists think some or all could have originated from what is called "Gain of Function".

In that theory, a certain type of virus can't jump from animal to human, such as Influenza B which can only infect humans. The scientists mutated this virus to infect rabbits, the virus is formed, and this can happen in nature. However, every time a virus mutates, it doesn't always move toward the "Gain of Function" or jump to a host that was immuned. The Secret labs are slowly tracing the viruses back through their mutations and back to their origin, to learn and manipulate these deadly diseases.

Hanna's thought process, a keen eye for detail, and the ability to see the whole picture, even though the parts are scattered, could see and feel where this research was going. She would not make a statement until she had all the damming facts. Hanna could see that the research had at least two hidden secret paths, none that was working on the research, and that the work being done may not be in the best interests of mankind. The more she uncovered the more she wanted to know, and it became an obsession with her. Hanna decided she would need help and shared her suspicions with her superiors in the hope of additional manpower.

Hanna went up the ladder with her preliminary findings and was granted the help and was informed that they may enlist outside help that the agency trusted. Hanna said she would welcome any assistance.

The agency put in a request for help on this alarming project, and even though they didn't have the facts and data to back up what they suspected, the Agency trusted Hanna's judgment and her expertise, and would go with it.

At the same time in Israel, the Mossad had been working on the same file and they were not into the theory or gave the research the same examination that the black ops did. The Mossad felt that the Red file was something that needed special attention, and their people were working on it, they just didn't have a Hanna working in their midst, but as usual, they weren't far behind, and at some point, the two agency's would have to share their files, and neither one liked that one bit. Again they would have to have a liaison that they all could and would trust, and they all could agree on. There are only three people that these two top secret agencies would agree on, but getting the three individuals onboard and to come out of their so-called retirement, may take a bit of doing, mostly because of the death threats against the three, and that at least two are on a list to get exterminated. The price tag on them is extremely high. If the two agencies could get the hits lifted or removed then maybe the two could be induced to work on the project. However, the agency knows that's impossible, because of the special secret worldwide hit squad. This is a sub-group of the Skull and Bones, and this double secret group is called Valhalla-(in Norse mythology, the hall of the Slain) It was employed by a previously known group that has been dismantled called the Ragnarok- in old Norse-(DOOM OF GODS AND MEN) and had paid in advance for their elimination. Virtually nothing could stop the proverbial hit, short of eliminating the whole group and that would be impossible. So a plan B would need to be implemented and the Black Ops knew how to accomplish that. It would be tricky but they have done it before and are confident they can do it again. It would require that the two individuals on the list be substituted with another two people who would seem to be eliminated or hit and who looked just like the targets, but the replacements would be agency people and they wouldn't be killed. At least that's the plan, and once the contract was fulfilled and paid the two people in question could go on with their life. No jeopardy, and that's what the secret Black Ops needed. They didn't want anyone actively looking for them so Plan B it was. In some cases, the hit squad knew of the Plan B and just let it go collected the cash, and showed the results of the hit.

Chapter 11

The Connection

Vonni received an email from Bjorne Jarvia that he would like to see her and Nate again soon, and said in the email that he may travel down to their neck of the woods for a visit, Bjorne had such a heavy lawyer responsibility and workload at all times and it was difficult to break free, however with the means of laptop computers and his extremely well versed and capable assistant attorneys he could take time away from the office and stay connected, and in an emergency be back in town within 12-15 hours.

Nate and Vonni were very happy that Bjorne would fly down to South America for a visit, but they both had reservations about the visit and replied their thought to Bjorn. His email reply was he needed to see them, and he thought it was urgent and couldn't relay his reasons via electronically. This reply made both Nate and Vonni go into heightened alert and sent a return email that they would love to have him come visit. All the while they were not at ease and would have to wait for the visit.

The Order of the Knights of Noah has been watching and electronically listening to Bjoern since they were hired by Damek Hava and have been assembling a file on everything that Meir Alter and his Grandson Bjoern did in the past. At the present, this group is investigating everything. So when Bjoerns sudden visit to South America came up, the group sent an associate to his office under the guise of a new client and asked to see Bjorne. He was told that he was out of the country. The associate from the Knights of Noah, Samual Briggs was told that this is normal because he and his company have dealing outside the country. He was informed that this was a special client and that Bjoern does a lot of international work, and his company would take Samual's Briggs information and as soon as Bjoern was back he would get in touch with him.

Bjoern's flight to South America was on a Boeing 777 X and this aircraft has state-of-the-art aerodynamics. The wings have an upward-curved angle from the root and downward toward the tips of the wings, which increases lift and reduces drag. In addition, this bird has wing tips that fold to increase wing span and also allow for the craft to enter most airports, such as category E Airports. The interior has been revamped over its predecessor with larger windows, just a bit smaller than the 787's windows and the inside is a wonder in itself, seating 426 passengers, and a range of approximately 7,285 miles, and a top speed of 682.87 mph, and this planes first class section is above all others.

During Bjoern's long flight to South America, unknown to him, he had a shadow that watched him from another section of the plane and seemed to be preoccupied with his laptop or was sleeping. This individual would record everyone that came in contact with his target. This shadow was assigned to tail Bjoern by his employer, the Knights of Noah, and he would hand Bjoern off figuratively speaking, at the airport to another operative that would carry on the surveillance once landed and they proceeded to his destination in Barichara and meet up with his friends Vonni and Nate.

Along with this trip and with Bjoern Tail there was another set of watchers that were in pursuit of a couple of targets that had a high price on their heads this other twosome didn't know that Bjoern had another tail, but this didn't matter to the two they were on a mission and quite motivated, and would stop at nothing to accomplish their task. They were sent by the now-disbanded Valhalla group and they had info that Bjoern was going to meet with the assignments. Unknown to these two assassins, was that the U.S. Black Ops were ready for the Valhalla's arrival and had almost everything in place just for them.

Vonni and Nate met Bjoern at the International Airport in Bucaramanga, and they exchanged pleasantries as old friends would, under the watchful eyes of the two groups that flew over on the same flight, and that had a unique interest in the three but in separate and distinct ways.

Black Ops wanted to keep Vonni and Nate alive, not only because of the service they did for the World but because of a new escapade or mission that the Black Ops and their superiors had lined up for these two, the individuals from Noah wanted Bjoern alive and they wanted the information or file that their principal wanted at all cost, and the Valhalla just wanted to do the hit and get the proof of their demise and collect the bounty that was placed on the two.

The three friends made their way from the airport back to Vonni and Nate's home in Barichara, and the last few miles of the trek were rough at best, and the only way in and out was by small vehicles or taxis or small Toyota pick-ups. Unknown to this re-united group of three they were being tailed by others, and the others had to stay at a safe distance. The black Ops knew about the hit twosome but not about the Noah group, and that was unusual because the Black Ops were aware of almost everything that was clandestine in their work zone. This Noah group was not, and never was on their radar. That's how secret this group is. The Noah group was hired to locate and retrieve the Red file that went missing, or was put in hiding at or just before Meir Alter's accidental death. This group didn't want Bjoern or his friends injured, so they watched. They could see these two other groups positioning up in their own ways to accomplish and complete their goals. The Noah group didn't know for sure what the Black Ops involvement was in Vonni and Nate. They sent out inquiries for information, however, the information they requested was not forthcoming because of the total top secrecy of these two, and the Noah Group didn't like loose ends, and made provisions for the Black Ops group and stayed clear of them, and just observed, waited and prepared for if and when the time was right, and the Red file came to the surface. That was the only skin in the game they had with the exception of the fact that they wanted Bjoern alive so he could lead the Noah group to the files. They would keep Bjoern healthy at all costs.

The Valhalla group just wanted the two targets eliminated and they had to do it in a way that wouldn't bring suspicion or major investigations. The Valhalla group had to use tack and they were masters at making deaths/hits look natural, so they would plan the hits out. They weren't the kind that made moves that weren't completely planned out to the last detail.

When the threesome arrived at Vonni and Nate's home, they settled in and made plans for dinner. During the time that Bjoern was picked up at the airport the nature of the trip was never discussed, mostly because of the secrecy that Bjoern thought he should keep. They went to dinner in town and they took a cab that was driven by one of the Valhalla assassins, he was all ears and said that he would be in the area for the return trip. This wasn't uncommon given that this town was small and business was slow. The driver's counterfeit name tag showed his name as Julio Gonzalez and he was indeed right there when dinner was complete.

Julio Gonzalez made quick friends with the threesome and explained that he and his partner were owners of an agency that does several different types of enterprise and that he could be their liaison for any outing or tourist adventures that they wanted, so they took his fake card in the event that they wanted his services.

Julio pulled up to Vonni's villa and dropped them off. In their driveway was a car that both Vonni and Nate knew. A sense of dread came over both of them. Of course, they didn't exhibit this feeling but the two's pulse rate jumped and they both went into heightened alert because they knew that this car and individual were never supposed to visit unless it was critical.

Vonni, Nate, and Bjoern entered their home, and sitting at the kitchen table was a Spanish sacerdotal, who is commonly referred to as Padre/priest. He was welcomed by Vonni and Nate. They both knew this was serious because this man sitting in front of them dressed in a holy man's garb was anything but a priest. They didn't let on and Bjoern wasn't the wiser, and the four were introduced. Vonni asked Preacher Guerrero if he would like some wine and he said he would, and they all sat down and talked. Preacher Juan Guerrero would ask Bjoern the usual questions, like how he liked Columbia so far. Juan would pry and try to get Bjoern to open up, and that's when Vonni would jump in and narrate the threesome's relationship, she would more or less put the inquisition to bed, and the conversation would resort to more benign topics. All the while Vonni and Nate were on edge and their adrenaline was pumped because he was their liaison, or handler as some would call him to the WWP, World Witness Protection System. Vonni knew that she and Nate would need to have a private conversation with the Padre, and this would need to be tonight.

Chapter 12

Damek Hava

Damek Hava is a proverbial ghost, as he was not known to many normal type people, although he was known to a few high-profile and mega-rich people and groups, and Damek was of course very much involved with his family, or his tribe, for lack of a better term, that was extensive and had several thousand and more if you follow the tree. He would watch over his own with extreme care. His people were all influential in their own right, and all were mega-rich, but didn't flaunt their wealth. They lived their lives as normal as most wealthy people do and stayed out of the spotlight completely. Damek was a real Patriarch, and the family never challenged his position. He of course is very unhappy about the Death of his best friend Meir Alter because Meir was the only outsider who knew of the long history of Damek and his large family. The two had been working together for decades. Meir was hand-picked for the position that he held because of Miers exceptionally high intellect in all areas, which rivaled Dameks intellect in many ways, but fell short in others.

Damek's last communication with Mier Alter was that a breakthrough had been made and that the formula and procedure were perfected on the task or mission that the two have been working on for several decades and the file number BOJ-25:33 was quite extensive and was missing, or at the very least hidden. Damek was for the first time in so many years, anxious, excited, and furious that he was so close to the long dream of his, the Fata Morgana that Damek chased, and was coming true, and that it was now out of his reach. Damek was not a person anyone wanted to be around during this kind of mood or mindset and his close assistants knew just how to manage these moments in time.

Damek finally settled down to a manageable level and started to work on the people who were working on the project that was so important to him. He would ask for and receive all the files that the labs had been working on with whatever results they had and the paths they were going on. However, this would be an uphill battle because Damek was coming in cold, and didn't have the vision or know the direction that his old friend was going. This whole episode and setback would just anger Damek beyond his so-called own boundaries. Damek had never been this mad, and this was new territory for him. He didn't like it and because it was foreign to him he didn't know how to handle it. The second thing that irritated Damek was that he didn't have a replacement for Meir in the wings or a protege, some because he couldn't and wouldn't trust anyone with the knowledge that he shared with Meir Alter. This setback could take decades if not more to solve. Meir Alter had such a great analytical mind and memory that he kept much of the scientific experiments and the processes committed to memory and would cross reference each one, part by part, molecule by molecule, and the exact amount of chemicals by weight that were used in each test along with the outcome, success, and failures. So a lot of the data wasn't in the file, but the end file had the process and chemicals, and every ingredient, listed for the final product. The project file BOJ-25:33 was tested over and over and confirmed to work perfectly and had no side effects. This process that Meir had worked on perfecting for his best friend Damek and his family was complete and the next part of the vocation would need to be set in motion. However, Damek's not having the file and procedure would mean a time delay, but on the upside, he knew that it could be done, and that made him happy.

Damek applied pressure on the secret investigation company to find and locate the BOJ-25:33 file and he also placed an enormous amount of pressure on the labs to find anything that Meir was more interested in than others. All the while these labs across the Globe were buying as many fetal stem cells as they could find legally, and as much as they could acquire any other way. The labs would pick and choose the type of stem cells and from what blood type. They would do a DNA test on each batch and sell off what they couldn't use. They were very specific on the blood type and the DNA sequence, and that order was given by Meir himself. So Damek left it in place because he thought that if Meir thought it was that important then he would as well.

The blood type that his labs coveted the most was (Rh-null) and for anyone who had this blood type and had an abortion, the stem cells from the blood type Rh-null were chronicled in their secret files for possible later use, The labs would also store and freeze many infant body parts that they would use for the secret experiment that the public or Government had no knowledge of. These labs across the world that Damek secretly controlled also worked on other projects. One project they would work on was that they have perfected a form of a virus-killing virus. They had a lot more testing to complete to adjust this particular virus so it would be selective, in that they want the lab-created virus to work on whatever they coded it for. As it is now it could eliminate most life-threatening viruses in a single dose or in some cases a couple of doses, and the results of that kind of elimination from the human body could be detrimental all at once. Dameks controlled labs also had the contracts to make the world's vaccines for every new and existing virus. They would produce the injections with the formula and dispersant agent, and the labs could at any time add to the formula additional chemicals that may be needed to keep the medicine fresh or for other purposes as deemed appropriate. These other additives would be listed and approved at the highest level. Little did the higher up know, that at any time a trojan horse could be added and was added. These new secret chemicals or vaccines that were added to the injections are benign while in their present form. The human body would absorb and store them in the muscle of the person who was injected with the compound. The chemical would stay in the body for life, similar to the worldwide vaccination that was administered to help the immune system develop immunity from disease and micro-organisms. These vaccines would stay active for life as a trojan horse that was in the medicine that came from Dameks labs. Again, the chemicals or ingredients are inert and waiting for the proper stimulant or secondary additive to complete the formula to make it whatever the end result or outcome was to be, and that day may never come.

The labs also secretly worked on cloning and experimented with every type of blood type, all under the direct supervision of Meir Alter, and Damek. It was now a new era in a new time with the true secret leader Damek, tasked to find a new individual to replace Mier. That was a tall order, because of the super-intellect that Mier had. Few people on the planet came close, and those who were in the same ballpark may not have the same outlook or insight that Mier had. Again, Mier was programmed by Damek for this project, and that took and required years. The loss of his friend and commandant was a setback that Damek was unprepared for, and that was not typical of him. The missing BOJ-25:33 red file angered

Damek to no end, almost to the point of making an error or mistake, and that was absolutely not part of his facade. Damek had the best of the best working on locating and the retrieval of the file BOJ-25:33, and he would have it at all costs.

Chapter 13

Bogata, Columbia

Vonni and Nate were having a nice quiet evening with Wine and hor d' oeuvres with their friends Bjoern, and the Padre, and as much as the foursome tried, and for the most part were successful at small talk, they all knew they had other pressing conversations with each other. The stress level for the Padre was increasing, as was for Vonni and Nate, because they were well aware of the importance and how critical the visit was from the holy man. However, they just couldn't break away from Bjoern and speak privately with him without raising suspicions, and in the same moment or instant Bjoern was also there for a pressing matter that he needed to speak to Vonni about. Vonni was aware of that as well and could tell and feel the tension and vibe, that this get-together should end soon, and that a separate meeting should and would occur. Vonni and Nate were more concerned about their handler Juan Guerrero the padre and why, out of the blue sky he came into the picture. They both knew it was not a good sign, and his presence put them in a state of stress that the two didn't like or want to be in. They knew the news he carried wasn't going to be good.

The Cocktail party ended and Vonni and Nate called a cab for Bjoern, before the cab arrived they set a time for them to meet again tomorrow and the three could go over business as it was. They explained to Bjoern that they had some town affairs to discuss with the preacher that they needed to discuss tonight and Bjoern understood and he was none the wiser.

The cab driver who picked up Bjoern at Vonni's house was none other than Julio Gonzalez, the same driver that dropped them off and the secret hit man from the Valihaha squad. This man was a professional and had his finger on the pulse of everything he could at all times, and spread cash around to get his job done. The dispatcher for the cab company was all too happy to accommodate Julio for a little extra folding money. He dropped Bjoern off at his hotel and had already done his homework on Bjoern and knew he was a non-player and wasn't a threat to his mission, but nonetheless he would keep a close eye on all possible problems. He left nothing to chance, and Bjoern was no different.

After the cab driver picked up Bjoern from Vonni and Nate's house, it was just the three of them and now the tension level rose. You could clearly see it on these two civilians' faces, almost to the point of panic. But they composed themselves and because the two have been through so much before this, and expected this day to come, their preparation or expectations for this day were planned, for but the actual day it arrives is almost more than you can handle. The two would need some time to get their wits together to meet this head-on, however, at this point the two needed to know all the details of the breach and the next plan of attack, if any, and what the protocol is. They may need to work all night with their handler and get ready to move on to greener pastures if needed. This saddened them because they made a life for themselves, and their absence would affect so many people.

Juan Guerrero, sat down with Vonni and Nate in the study, but not until he scanned for listening devices or what is called bugs. He then set up a jamming or signal diffuser in the room to scatter any sound or conversation they had so long/short range listening dishes couldn't be deployed. Some may think this was overkill, but Juan knew who he was dealing with and no amount of precaution was enough. Once Juan was satisfied he was in a silent and secure room he would begin his briefing. Both Vonni and Nate sat and waited for the ritual to get completed because they knew just how dangerous the situation was, and the time this required was taking its toll on them. Juan could tell and advised them to have another bottle of wine, at which time the two were all too happy to indulge in.

The wine bottle was opened and Juan declined a glass after he started with his explanation as to his presence in their life at this time. They knew when that happened it was serious. He went on and told them of the breach in the program, that their cover was blown, and that besides the cover being blown, he had another proposition or mission that he would hope that they consider once this problem is dealt with. Juan said first things first though, let me tell you where we're at, what is happening, and what I'm going to do to rectify the situation as it is. The problem as both of you are aware of, is that there is a bounty on your heads that has not been paid and is worldwide. Of course, several hunter groups have been looking for you two on and off since the time the bounty/hit was issued, and now a group or should I say a twosome has located you and they are in the area and have been watching you and planning their mission. This takes time and they need to make it look like an accident if at all possible or as close to one, and that's where I come in. Juan went on to explain his plan and how he would proceed. He knew who the two assassins were and what they looked like, and they didn't know him so that was good for the plan.

The beginning of the plan would go as follows they discussed it and went over it several times, and both Vonni and Nate rehearsed their dialog in order, and were able to act it out perfectly, and they would ad-lib if necessary. The two of them knew that they had only one shot at this and if they weren't 100 % convincing the whole mission would deteriorate and the two assassins would terminate them on the spot, or as quickly as possible, and not be concerned with covering up the murder.

The plan was that Vonni, Nate, and the Padre would call and hire a cab to town for lunch, Padre Juan knew that the driver would be Julio Gonzalez, and during the ride, they would talk about a pending trip to Bogota, Columbia and that they will need an aircraft for transportation. They would discuss the airport they would fly out of and the charter service they would use, and the whole time Julio would take a mental note. In his mind, he already started his plan for the termination of his targets. Julio had no qualms about collateral damage, or in this case additional deaths. Vonni per her script stated that she had some legal work to perform and Nate said he would like to visit some of his missionary colleagues who worked at the many orphanages in the area, the Padre said he would see them off and that he couldn't make the trip, during the cab ride, the driver Julio piped in that he knows the airfield very well and when they are ready please call him directly and he gave them his personal card, almost like an Uber service but it was simply cab service on demand, Julio said he would set aside the necessary time for the trip since he knew that date and time, and they all agreed and the first part of the planned scenario was set.Juan Guerrero was kind of happy, but he didn't trust anything and left nothing to chance, a true skeptic at his core, but he was pleased with how his personal charges performed, and now he would need to put plan B into place because he didn't know exactly how Julio was going to complete his mission but he had a general idea, going by the past hits these very professionals had done before, plus Juan just narrowed the ways to cover up the killings, and he was sure in his mind just how the assassins would go about it, and that's where plan B would come into play, and the planning for this caper would require a large amount of money and about seven days to set up, however, Juan wasn't new to the area and had contacts and people that he could trust.

The plan was now on and going forward and both Vonni and Nate were extremely nervous but they concealed it well.—So they wait—

Chapter 14

SEARCH FOR FILE~ BOJ~25:33

Damek has increased his search effort for the BOJ-25:33 file and his search team Noah was ordered to put more people on the case. The secrecy protocol was lifted somewhat, and that secrecy protocol was to keep or conceal the identity, and the existence of Damek. He has always been the proverbial ghost, and the real power behind the leaders of the world, silent in most cases and applying pressure where needed. Damek and his extremely large and wealthy family have the means and influence to make or break just about anyone or any government. Dameks family tree goes back, let's say, farther than any other in history, and the numbers are staggering. Plus the combined wealth of this virtually unknown connected family is off the charts. If and when Damek makes a decision as family head the rest fall in line. Because of the patriarchal style of leadership, he has enlisted his family to work on and secretly search for the lost file, and they will coordinate their efforts through him. Because Mier Alter was a global traveler and was present in many countries the search for the very important BOJ-25:33 file would be worldwide. This file was so important to the Damek family, and they all knew that it was important but not how much. That was a secret left to the Patriarch Damek. He didn't want his family to know just how important it was, however, they knew him well enough to know that when he enlisted them all it was important, and virtually unprecedented. The last time this order or request was made was when the clan or family was ordered, on the absolute need to evacuate their homeland and migrate to the other parts of the world that they all decided was best for them, and what was safest for them all. This call to assembly, or order by the Patriarch was not taken lightly. His extremely large family knew that Damek was working on a method or cure for the plague that only affected their own, and that as a family if this cure or actual procedure wasn't found, that as a family they would all slowly pass away, this plague or defect as it really was, had a time element or what may be called an expiration date on his people. Again they knew Damek had been working on an elixir, or some other sort of family-saving cure, and that this worldwide communication with the family could mean only one thing. That was that there was a new cure to their demise. So they all in their own way started the search. They had to do it with the top secrecy that they have always kept. However, with so many family members getting active, this movement could trigger a world intel flag with many secret government agencies. The file was so important to Damek that he would risk exposure and worry about the fallout later. The very survival of his family was the most important thing, and Damek had the means and influence to cover up almost any international intelligence investigation.

The family started their own research with the coordination of a new liaison of Dameks with whom he has worked for years. Through various buffers, this new coordinator has never met Damek and never will, and has only communicated with him by secure phone. As it is no one other than Damek's family and one non-family member has ever met him or even knows what he looks like. Meir Alter was the only non-family member to ever meet Damek, and the only person outside the clan that knew Damek's history all the way back to Damek's beginnings. Mier was the only person to whom he trusted the health and well-being of his family to. Meir was so smart and loyal, again his only intellect rival was Damek and the difference was that Meir had a thought process that Damek didn't possess when it came to his research. That very process has always eluded Damek even being the most intelligent man on the planet. Without this particular process, instinct, or the way Meir assembled the information, Damek could never have made the leap or seen the big picture. None of his family had that ability that most great researchers have, and that's why Damek knew at an early time that he would need outside help. His search for these unique people took time, and then he had to make sure the individuals who had the intellect could and would work with him, and that he could trust them. This process took a long time before Damek found Meir Alter, and he could see that this was a match. The second part of the equation for someone to assist Damek was that this person needed to have certain other qualities, and that was the longevity of life. Damek could see or feel if an individual had that long life gene, that so many people inherited, but the unique combination of long life and superior intellect was even more rare, and when a person could pass those criteria they would be conditioned from their early youth to young adults and again tested to see if the candidates could pass the threshold of becoming the lead scientist and researcher for the Damek group, few people reached the top level of consideration, or that met all the requirements, and when one did the final test was if they bought into what Damek and his family secret research were all about. Part of the buy-in would be the total loyalty to Damek and his family without reserve, and do whatever it required to accomplish the difficult and seemingly impossible task asked of them and that was to cure or reverse the effects of the plague/defect that the Damek family has been afflicted with. So far there was only one person who reached all levels of the daunting task at hand. And that was Meir Alter, and Damek treated him like family. Even though Meir wasn't blood family he was as close as any in so many ways that it was uncanny. This phenomenon occurred in others, but in much less degrees, and Meir had almost the same attributes as one of Dameks blood family.

The Damek family's private search for information and the location of the said BOJ-25:33 file didn't go unnoticed and the world was buzzing with the secret intelligent systems. These secret services that watched and kept files on everything that they considered, may be a threat now or in the future, didn't like the fact that for the most part, they were flat-footed in this case. And had to play catch up, anytime someone or something was being sought after. Especially in this magnitude, the intel community took notice, and the worldwide family search did just that.

During the family inquiry into the lost or hidden BOJ-25:33 file, the Damek family would do the usual search for Meir Alter's relatives, and they located only one surviving and that was his grandson Bjoern Jarvis the search also showed that he just made a trip to South America to visit friends, and now the researchers would locate and investigate who he was with and why, and this whole investigation would put additional pressure on the Padre or black OPs agent Juan Guerrero as he would get a daily briefing on the search. Juan didn't know what the connection was between his two charges and Bjoern, but Juan didn't like mysteries and would soon get to the bottom of the questions he had, and the answers would make his task and job a lot more difficult.

Chapter 15

The Plane Trip

In the coming days, Padre Juan quickly put together the airplane trip from the city of Bucaramanga which was 34.3 miles away from the town of Barichara. He had a plan that he had used in the distant past to help him cover his tracks and the airfield that the aircraft would take off from was the Bucaramanga (BGA). Commercial flights would take about one hour but he enlisted a twin prop Cessna 404 Titan, this particular bird has a ceiling of 26,000 feet and a top speed of 266 mph, a range of more than 1,000 miles, and seats 7 people plus 1 crew. The reason was that he could manipulate the flight path and leave the airfield when they wanted versus the commercial airlines. With this aircraft and the owners that Padre Juan has done business with many times in the past, and he was able to use his own pilot and crew. The smaller but perfectly sized plane would do exactly what was required for the next phase of his dark mission.

The plan was set and part two was next. Juan would set that part in motion when he orchestrated the whole thing and went over the acting that both Vonni and Nate would again have to perform. They would all go to dinner again using the cabby, Julio Gonzalez, whom they now have his personal cell phone number, and knew he was one of the hit men for Noah. They informed Julio that they would need his services for a cab ride to the city of Bucaramanga in two or three days, Julio said it was no problem and inquired as to what aircraft service or company they would be using they told him the name and Julio would do his usual do diligence on this phase of his plan and investigate the company and aircraft they would use and the pilot if one was chosen at this time, Julio is a professional and left nothing to chance and no loose ends. All bases were covered and his partner in crime back in the States Samual Briggs was doing back up for him and in constant communication. When everything checked out to Julio's satisfaction and he was sure that he was safe in the next phase, he had two days minimum to set up his plan for the hit, in a place and for it to look like an accident, or at least, some sort of malfunction that would be almost impossible to investigate.

That night Julio sat in his apartment at his work table/desk and performed his magic, with electronics and wires, fuses, and batteries, and the C-4, explosive would be installed last and was stored on another table for safety, even though this type was very safe Julio still kept safety first, he would assemble a small bomb with 1.1/4 lbs of C-4 more than enough to do the job, and he hooked up an altitude proximity fuze that he can set at the precise altitude he wants and that will be determined by the flight plan that will be placed, and with that Julio can tell exactly where the plane will be, and over the mountainous region between Bucaramanga and Bogota, and this area would be so desolated that search and recovery would take several weeks or not at all. The height or altitude of the plane at the time of ignition would be seen on radar. As the plane's transponder was on the radar blip would be on and in an instant, it would be off and all communication would cease, and quite possibly another aircraft close by or someone on the ground would see the explosion and radio or contact the authorities. However sighting from the ground was not high because of the terrain and mountains, density.

The next issue was to get the device on the aircraft undetected and before they took off or at the time of departure and that part would be worked out before lift-off, Julio worked into the night on his little project and tested it several times and it worked flawlessly, the size of the package was about as big as a cigar box maybe just a little larger and much heavier, because of the electronics and batteries and of course the 1-1/4 pound of plastic explosive. Julio made his device look like an ELT, emergency locator transmitter, he removed all the electronics from a working unit and replaced them with his own creation. Because it was standard equipment for the plane it didn't look out of place. These devices are normal for aircraft to have in them. This beacon would light up and emit a radio signal in the case of a planes emergency landing, for the authorities to find you and send help. It was a mandatory piece of equipment especially down in South America where the Jungle and mountains are so prevalent, and no emergency landing areas.

The stage was set, the device was ready and the night before Vonni and Nate were to depart on their trip, Julio was at the airport installing this device, under the watchful eyes of one of Juan Guerrero's black Ops people. Everything was going as planned, the trip was set and the hit was going to be done.

The night before their departure the Padre Juan had another impromptu meeting with Vonni and Nate. Since the three of them were as thick as thieves and were all in on the mission at hand, the Padre had a serious potential problem that he needed to discuss with the two. They sat down early in the evening and Juan went over the twist in the plan, if it was a twist Juan wasn't sure just yet. Juan started the conversation/briefing with the Bjoern Jarvia issue and both Vonni and Nate looked at the Padre in what would be a look of getting completely caught off guard and they were both on high alert. Juan went on to explain that as their handler and protector, he ran a background check on Bjoern and he received a cryptic response. One that put him on edge and in his businesses as a black ops person, that took some doing. The response or cryptic file/briefing he received was that there was a secret blackout worldwide search for all relatives of a man called Meir Alter and that Bjoern's name came up, a blackout search means quiet and no leaks just a person of interest, but the Padre knew better this was not just a name or persons whereabouts search as indicated. This was a find and detain and or retrieve and take into custody. Actually, it was an order to pick him up unharmed at all cost, kidnap, and bring Bjoern to whoever ordered the retrieval, the Padre knew from past experience that this was not a good sign and the added people looking at all three of them was not going to help the situation, this whole mission just got a lot more difficult. The Padre Juan explained the situation to them and shared some of the briefings that weren't classified and said that because of Bjoern's presence in the mix, the plans would have to change, however, the timeline for the coming events could not, the next plan of attack was to get Bjoern onboard with everything that will happen in the next 24 hours and that would mean that they would have to reveal much of their past to him. They would have to convince him that his participation in the plan was not open for discussion and that he had no choice. Because not only are Vonni and Nate's lives in jeopardy, but Juan thinks that Bjoern's may be as well. They called Bjoern and made arrangements for him to come over to Vonni's and Nate's Villa and Juan sent his own transportation so that Julio the cab driver was unaware of this visit. When Bjoern arrived at the Villa the three sat down and had some wine and they all settled in, that's when Vonni took first control of the meeting and explained that she and Nate had a problem and that Bjoern may inadvertently become part of it, at that point she turned the discussion over to the Padre, a man that portrayed a quiet Holy man and preacher. When he now spoke he was anything but, he was a man in control, decisive, and just short of a bully. He took control of the conversation and more or less didn't let anyone speak until he was finished and at that time he would have the Q&A. Juan explained the situation of the witness protection for both Vonni and Nate and said he would go into the details of why they were in the program a little later, he explained that the two were in grave danger because of a standing hit or assassination placed on them some years ago. Bjoern sat there as an attorney would and listened and put together his own thoughts and questions for the time when he was allowed to ask. However, before the Q&A Juan went on to explain that there was a worldwide search for him(Bjoern) and that Juan was trying to discreetly get more information on why. This new revelation of the search for him, caught Bjoern completely by surprise he wondered who would want him that bad, especially in Black Ops. Mostly because he has never done anything outside the law or anything covert for or against the government, and that's when it hit him. Could it be because of the files that his grandfather had hidden in the rental house, and if it was what could possibly be in those files that are that important that these secret Dark intel agencies are looking for him? Bjoern recalled what he read in the file from his grandfather and this opened the door a little, and shed some light in a way for him to understand or comprehend what was happening. However, Bjoern still did not have a full grasp of the severity of his situation, or the magnitude of involvement his Grandfather had in any of this, however, that was about to change.

They took a small break from what was a tense and overwhelming speech that Juan presented and the three were wobbled in their almost always stable lives. Something that was not a norm for any of them. They liked being in control, and with this new twist in the state of affairs for them, it took its toll. They would need time to absorb and process what they have heard so far.

Chapter 16

Black Ops Researcher Hanna Torres

Hanna is one of the most extraordinary researchers that the Black Ops Intel agency has ever had. Because of her incredible intellect, she should never have been in the research department of this agency. She is clearly overqualified for the position, let alone for government work. But Hanna loved her work and always thought she could make a difference, and that's why she elected to accept the job offer when she was approached.

Her continued research on the file she was working on kept getting more interesting and more complicated. The work or experiments that were being performed in the secret parts of the many labs across the world, using stem cells, research, virology, DNA, and blood type research was staggering. Hanna had file after file of information from these labs, and she in her unique and abstract way of thinking, and with the type of mind that could and would put multiple pieces of a puzzle, or in this case multiple files and experiments together, she would see a connection or path between one to another in a way that no other person could. Some people would call it bread crumbs, some would say that if you pulled on a thread at the bottom of a wool sweater the whole thing would unwind a little at a time and you could get to the beginning or core. In any event, once Hanna got on the scent of a mission she was like a pit bull that would lock on and never let go.Because she was such a highly qualified researcher with a bachelor's degree in Biologic, and had vast experience in other fields, with her way of looking at puzzles and complex files, she was starting to get a little excited by what she was uncovering. She also knew that this unraveling that she was trying to do would take an unknown amount of time and man-hours. She also knew it would be worth the cost, but was unsure what the end results would be. She could be chasing a ghost, but her instincts told her differently, and her supervisors would go along with her for a while, but they would need something more concrete than a Hanna hunch, or intuition. She had a mountain of files and a limited amount of researchers to assist her, and these other researchers didn't have the eye for detail that Hanna Torres had. She found that she would have to go over the work of the others and that redundancy in man hours was counterproductive. Hanna would have to show something to the higher-ups that would make them want to approve additional funds for the research and maybe better help.

Hanna's uncommon thought process with the files and her long hours would be fruitful as she would put together a brief that she could corroborate with facts. That the labs were working, independently of each other, but unknown to each other they were all working on the same experiments and they were in different phases of their conclusion to the tests. Because they all were doing it with different formulas or procedures and techniques, but the outcome they were all looking for was the same.

Hanna could see on the edges that several of the tests had the nuances that other labs had using blood, virus, stem cells, and DNA testing all in the same research. The same but different, she could see that at some point these labs looked at and made records of cloning. She could not find any more testing in that area, but felt that they were still working in that area. The amount of data that her department has is staggering. Hanna knows that she is just touching the tip of the iceberg and that she is completely overwhelmed by paper. Even with the use of the giant computers they had at their disposal, the paper trail Hanna was following couldn't be done in the same way she does it, so Hanna would have to do it hands-on or find a program that had her unique thought process. To Hanna's experience and knowledge that device doesn't exist, so she works on one file after another.

The search for the owner or owners of the labs came up empty or showed owned by investors and that was a surprise because the agency of Black Ops could almost always find that information. That bit of information put up a red flag and was noted in the growing red file that Hanna was forming.

No other worldwide intel agency was doing the same research that Hanna was involved with. That gave them a leg up. Mostly because when others started looking around, that's when the information that Hanna was getting out of these labs would slow or stop, and she didn't want that. The labs were also tasked with other experiments that were not a top secret and they would let out that they were trying to make a product to cure any of many other known diseases or inflictions. They would manufacture the vaccines that were shipped around the world for the flu and so many other viruses, and these vaccines were made under the strict guidelines of the WHO. These vaccines were bought and paid for by this organization for distribution. The vaccines would be tested by another lab that was controlled by the one and only Damek and because he was never on a board of directors or a CEO or affiliated with the labs in any way there wasn't a conflict of interest, and the vaccines could have whatever Damek's labs wanted in them.

Hanna found that some of the secret labs were working on what is called,

"Gain Of Function" research. Which means juicing up naturally occurring animal viruses in a lab to make them more infectious among humans. This is not new and has been going on for a long time. The files that Hanna has from the secret labs are not always complete because they are acquired by means that are not legal. So she would request additional information from the people that they have in place and that would take time because the files of information weren't always easy to access. Hanna could see a pattern that no one else saw, and the more information she received the better the picture was. However, the end game was beyond Hanna's vision, she just knew that it was big, and dangerous and thought, or felt that it needed to be researched. She would put her brief together and present it up the ladder, Hanna would have to present the brief in person and explain her findings in lay terms so her superiors could grasp the severity of her research so far. They would have to make a decision on the next steps if any.

What Hanna didn't know was that the agency had some inkling of the labs in question work and the dangers involved. That's why they put Hanna on the case. To authenticate what some other researchers had discovered, but not to the same degree that Hanna has or with as many facts. With this new material and backup information they advised Hanna that they would get back to her with their decision for funds for additional research, however, they had already made up their minds that they would fully fund it. They just weren't sure where Hanna was going to fit in. She was so gifted and they knew she would be a great asset to the next level of the research team. They also knew that time was never on their side. The Hanna issue, if you want to call it an issue, would be if the advanced group of investigators would accept her on the team. This could be a problem and would be at the consideration of them. The next group is quite good and linking another unknown person to them may be difficult and would have to be accepted by this tight group, and that could be a tall order. That group is in South America fighting for their lives.

The Agency put everything in motion as to the final research team goes. But the Black Ops didn't have confirmation that this special team would work for them or come out of retirement so they covered the bet, kept Hanna in the wings, and let her think that they were just considering the missions funding. Hanna had no idea that the powers that be, had another plan going.

The Dark Ops Agency made contact with their field operative through coded message and found that he was well on his way for the planned mission called "To Kill a Mother Bird", not to be mistaken by the book, and he informed the Agency that he had to make some last-minute changes in the mission.He would send the encrypted file to them with all the players and the timelines and explain why a new player was now among them. The Agent would also inform the Agency that he was not one hundred percent sure the new teammate was onboard with the mission and will keep them advised.

The Agency didn't like new people on their missions, first Hanna, now another individual that they will look at when the file is received, the Agency was not amused with the field agent adding someone without confirmation, this was not how the Agency was run and quite unorthodox and the field agent better have a good reason.

Chapter 17

Professor Shume

In Israel Professor Shume, as the Professor was referred to by the University students, has been keeping a close watch on the intel that has secretly been going back and forth across the Globe. Shume has some insider connections with the Israeli intel, and because he was a semi-retired agent he had access to more than most. The intel Shume received was that his good friends Vonni and Nate may have been located and that the assassins were on their way, and may already have a line on their targets. He wanted to reach out to his friends, and he had the means and would do so this morning in a coded cryptic way that only Vonni and Nate would understand. Shume sent a long e-mail to his friends. In the e-mail, he would talk about mundane things and about such things as other family and friends. Near the end of the e-mail was the code that would alert Vonni and Nate that their cover was indeed blown. In the event that they didn't believe Padre Juan the code words are, "wish you were here", and in context with other incidentals and well wishes. The e-mail would end and Vonni and Nate recognized what the code meant and it reinforced what they already knew. The need to relocate and escape was now more pressing. They shared the e-mail with Juan. He said he didn't know they were still in contact with Shume, and the fact that the hit was now listed on the international dark intel web and was going to be completed bothered Juan. He thought he had a little more time and privacy than what he just learned. As of now, Juan knew that more eyes were watching and he would need to make sure that phase 2 was cleaner and more precise than he originally planned. That was a problem of sorts but just a timing issue, and he would handle that easily. He made the changes in the mission and that was that.

Professor Shume was on top of everything that was going on in the world's dark intel system and he watched the closely guarded top-secret search for an individual, Bjoern whom Shume wasn't aware of or had heard of before. But that this person Bjoern was in the general vicinity of Vonni and Nate were, and that bothered him. He wondered why the search, and what the secret group Noah wanted with this man called Bjoern. The Professor didn't like coincidences and the fact that this Bjoern was as close to his friends set off internal alarms inside him. That fact made him want to get involved and travel to South America.

Professor Shume and Padre Juan have come across each other in the past and were at best just acquaintances, but they knew each other's job and respected each other. Foreign spies seldom become good friends because they have different agendas, but if they are on the same respective teams they would provide the respect that each would need, and be as honest as they could be without telling or revealing any secrets.

Vonni responded to Professor Shume that she received his e-mail and in her response, she replied, that she wished she was there as well and that was the correct response, for she and Nate are in good hands. In her e-mail, she mentioned her friend whom she hadn't seen for a long time, and referred to her friend just as Bjoern, and that this friend was with them and was going to stay for a while. That was a coded message to the Professor that Bjoern was in trouble as well and that all was going as planned.

The Professor knew that Bjoern was in South America because of the dark intel but he was not aware that Bjoern knew or was close to Vonni and Nate and that he was part of what was called the extraction of witnesses. This would set Shume off on what was a storm of research on his end to quietly look at and monitor the situation that was unfolding in Vonni's world. The professor's hands were tied because if he tried to intervene he could completely upend what Juan had in place, and Shume was confident that the Padre was capable of making phase 2 go through without a hitch. The professor would have to sit and be a spectator on this one and that was not where he liked to be. Shume always had his hands in the mix and controlled everything, and the fact that he had to watch was more stress than he had had in the last couple of years. Sitting on the sidelines being benched was never a place the Professor had been and he had to watch from afar and see how it unfolds.

The professor, in his ultimate wisdom and long career in the intel community didn't like the fact that Vonni, Nate, and a newcomer Bjoern were in trouble and that this new player Bjoern was someone he didn't know or have intel on. Anything he would do on the intel stage to find info on Bjoern would set up red flags so he would have to resort to the dark web. Shume knew that wasn't secure and he didn't like his hands being tied like this the Professor was a man who always had more than enough information and in this case, he was nearly empty-handed and that gave him fits.

Professor Shume is so well connected to the dark intel system, and Mossad and could be activated into service at a drop of the hat. Because he was so well versed in almost everything interesting going on, the powers that could send him into the field again knew he was prepared. The Professor was silently gearing up for what he thought was an imminent assignment that would involve Vonni and Nate. The professor didn't know at this time when or if he would be sent into service, but his intuition and long experience in the intel Society gave him the feeling that he would be drafted back in, and that made him feel good. He missed the old days when he was an active member of the Mossad, and not the backup he is now. In any event, he was getting his passports in order and other gear that he would need. He thought that he may be sent to South America to address the Vonni and Nate position and he was as ready as can be.

The professor received his encrypted orders to go and assist his long friends in South America with standing orders to get on location with any additional agents he thought he would require. He was to observe and make ready, but not to intervene in any way as the Americans seemed to have it under control. The Mossad would stay out of foreign internal issues for the most part, but if the Mossad could make any connection with any affair affecting them and Israel, they would send a small group to be in a position to protect their interests if it came up. In most cases the deployment of these mini-groups of agents that monitored whatever they were sent to watch, they were on target and being at ground zero during the beginning of a bad operation. The Mossad didn't like being left out in the cold or being caught flat-footed. Their agency was so good and so in tune with world events and with their agents all across the world. This intel group was either deep in the matter or have influence in the outcome and this trip to South America was no different, just getting in position.

The professor would of course change his identity and the way he looked with different features, such as a beard and or graying hair, the usual disguise that would be used during these common and often nonissue trips. Shume would leave for South America in the morning and arrive there the next day, he wouldn't be in a position near where Vonni and Nate lived for another two days and may miss them entirely.

The professor was not privy to the plans of Padre Juan. And when that plan is put into action. The Professor would read between the lines and know what had just happened and he would make his next move accordingly. He would stay out of the mission until the dust settled. Professor Shume would monitor everything and make his moves in a given time, because Shume knew that his agency was not the only one watching this. He had intel on them all but didn't have any photos of the other players and that was not a deal breaker because Shume was used to that kind of Skullduggery.The Professor thrived in this kind of environment, and was more at home than any other agent. The professor was and is a natural at what he does. In this case, he knew the players Vonni and Nate that he was sent to help, and this group trusted him because of a previous mission the three had been on.

Chapter 18

The Assassination

All three Vonni, Nate, and Bjoern, listened to what Padre Juan had to say. After some discussions about what they had just been told, they knew that at least Vonni and Nate's lives were in danger, and that was a fact. The revelation that Bjoern was being tracked down by a secret group called the Knights of Noah, put him in a state that Bjoern had never been in or felt before. First that he was being hunted and he didn't know why, and number two he didn't know for sure what this group's intentions were. The Padre Juan was not much help because the agent knew of this group's past and its methods along with the results of some of their searches. In almost all of this group's involvements, the targets didn't survive and Juan didn't think this time would be any different at least from what info he has at this point. This group's normal terminations of its targets led the handler to believe that this one would be the same and he conveyed this to his now three charges, and that he could adjust his phase two plan to include Bjoern. But that it would be a little tricky and the three would need to play-act in the cab and convince the hitman cab driver Julio that all was still safe, this man Julio was extremely cautious and could read between the lines so the threesome would need to do the acting well, almost award-winning.

The three entered Julio's cab early morning of the fateful day. The weather was the usual clear and sunny and the temperature was in the 70's. As was the norm for this time of year in this part of Columbia. For aircraft, this is considered perfect flying, and the term that most pilots use is the skies are severe clear and the winds are good, with no crosswinds or wind shears. So their flight from Bucaramangas airport to Bogota and commercial flights take about one hour, this aircraft was much slower but could land in smaller airfields and again was better for picking the time of departure. While they were on the way to the airport, everyone sitting in the cab knew what was planned and no one spoke the truth. For Julio, it was a payday, and for Vonni and Nate, it was another new beginning. One the two didn't especially like but knew was necessary and they both knew was coming. What these two didn't know was that from this point in time, their lives would change again. Just like it did several years ago and the two would be tapped with another job that would be as dangerous as the last time. This would be just as important. The next few weeks or months would be more stressful and dangerous than the last time, and the revelation from what the two would learn soon would be beyond their comprehension.

Bjoern's entry into the mix with the cab driver was explained that he was a friend who was visiting from out of the country and that both Vonni and Nate talked their friend Bjoern into coming along. The charade was going as well as expected, and the driver Julio was more or less just listening to the conversations going on and looking for anything that he felt was out of the norm, or a red flag that would alert him that his cover had been blown. So far the three had play acted well together and the ride to the airport went uneventful.

Julio removed the baggage from the trunk and collected his fee and a generous tip and he wished them a good trip, all the time feeling pretty good about the payday and the amount he would receive for the hit. After Julio dropped them off he went to a coffee shop and opened his laptop and dialed in a couple of apps for his viewing. He would watch the news on his laptop for anything that was current, and on another app, this one was quite dark and secret. This app was able to monitor and watch the location of a given cell phone or phones, and the app could do this without the owner's consent. The cell tower pings were accurate in most cases to within several feet, however in the mountains and jungle the accuracy was not that good, but could be watched from his computer. Again, because of the scarce cell towers between these two cities in Columbia, the accuracy may well be several miles. However, that wasn't a concern to Julio, all he wanted to see and monitor was the general flight path on the GPS screen and the eventual termination of the pings from the phone to the tower and he could watch the exact time the pings went offline.

The aircraft was loaded with luggage in the bays and the passengers, were just the three of them plus the crew. Vonni, Nate, and Bjoern all sat in their seats and made ready for the flight and they taxied down the ramp going through the safety check and engine spool up, just getting prepared for the beginning of the flight. They received clearance to depart and the aircraft lined up on the runway and spooled up the engine with the brakes applied. At a given time the aircraft was cleared for take-off and the craft slowly moved down the runway picking up speeds. As it reached take-off speed the plane would rotate, or the nose would lift off and then the rest of the bird, and from that point, the aircraft would pick up speed. When it reached a certain altitude they would retract the landing gear and again that would help the speed, and angle of attack airborne. The pilot spoke with the tower and requested the ok to turn to their heading that was listed on the flight path. They were given the ok, as the plane continued to climb to the designated altitude before leveling off to stay in the correct air separation between other planes. Once airborne, the pilot entered their vector and continued on and grabbed altitude to get over the mountains that they would need to transverse between the two destinations.

Located in the rear of the plane was the altered ELT Emergency locator transmitter that Julio had made special for this flight, the transmitter was in the exact position that it was when Julio installed it in the dead of night, Julio had removed all the electronics from the box and replaced them with his own and that included the special altitude proximity sensor activator and C-4 and the special battery that would hold a charge for a long time without being hooked up to power.

The flight path took them close to the Andes mountain and they had to climb to an elevation of over 12,000 feet. At that altitude the pilots were required to use their oxygen and the passengers did not. The flight plan showed that they would reach 14,000 feet so they could pass over the highest point or mountaintop and not experience wind shear, the Cessna 404 twin was capable of about 26,000 feet and they would not come close to that altitude. What the Cessna 404 pilot did was squawk the transponder code that was assigned to them. From their departing airports pilot may be required to squawk a given code by an air traffic controller, via the radio using the phrase such as Cessna -n-number-Squawk 0366. The pilot then selects the 0366 code on his transponder and the track on the air traffic controller's radar screen will light up with that number and the controller will be able to identify that aircraft for the duration of the flight. This code is unique to this aircraft during this time, and once the plane lands the squawk number is terminated and can be reassigned, over and over again. The Cessna 404 would go above and sometimes behind the mountain range and the radar signature would be lost and this is normal if there wasn't an emergency declared, radar is a line of site.

Shadowing the Cessna 404 that has the special passengers of Vonni, Nate, and Bjoern, and flying lower than the radar can pick up was another smaller but extremely quick aircraft that was not rated at 26,000 feet but could easily traverse the 12-14,000 foot ceiling that the 404 presently cruising at. This ghost plane was being flown by remote control and the operators of the controls were in a third plane, that had Padre Juan and some of his agents, and they would monitor the flight.

When the Cessna 404 was approaching the site or given area that Juan had chosen the bird would position itself behind a mountaintop top and the tower would lose radar contact with the transponder. At this time the 404 would shut down its squawk box, and the ghost plane that had its squawk box dialed into that frequency would turn it on and emerge from behind the obstructing mountain. At that time the Cessna 404 would dive or descend below the ranges of the mountain and completely be radar invisible. The remote-controlled Ghost plane under the guidance of the chase plane would emerge and continue on, and the tower controller wouldn't know a switch had been made. The 404 made a 180-degree turn and dropped down into the valley between the mountains, and its new destination was a remote dirt/grass landing strip airport, that was a couple of hundred miles from the point where the switch had been made.

The replacement aircraft would fly the given flight plan and when this remote-controlled ghost plane reached a certain altitude that was set for the 404 Cessna's and was clearly picked up in the tower radar the ghost aircraft was now squawking the Cessna transponders number and the transition went unnoticed. At about 2,000 feet above the mountain top or approximately 14,000 feet, the ELT Emergency locator transmitter was set to deploy and ignite, however, the altered ELT was removed from the Cessna 404 long before lift off and this new ghost craft had its own remote destructive devise in the back seat, and would be activated by the chase plane some miles away. The chase plane was in the line of sight of the ghost plane but well under the radar scope, so even though the chase plane didn't Squawk any frequency it was not seen. When the ghost plane was on the radar screen for several minutes the chase plane simply activated the internal bomb and the ghost plane signature just blipped off the screen. This set off a warning in the control tower and the controller, started to call the 404 over and over. After a short time, he requested help from any other planes in the area if they had a visual of the 404. The controller repeated his call out and requests to other planes in the area when he received a return transmission from an airliner that was about 10,000 feet higher than the Cessna 404. The pilot reported that he and his co-pilot saw what appeared to be an explosion, and gave the tower an approximate GPS setting. The controller would ask the airline pilot what they saw, and the reply was that it looked like an aircraft had blown up. Possible engine failure or decompression, but the distance between the two was too great to confirm the planes N-number or type of craft, but could see that it was going down in flames and in several pieces. A search and rescue team could not be at the crash site for several days or longer because of the remote location of the debris field, and a helicopter would not be able to land in the mountain area or make a round trip because of the distance and fuel consumption just getting over the mountains. So the search and rescue would be performed by land and the prospects of survivors were low, because of the description of the explosion and the fact that the aircraft came apart at high altitude, a search plane would be sent with cameras and slow flight could be done and that would just locate the crash site and if any survivors were present. They may signal the small search plane. Again, the prospect of finding anyone alive was low.

Julio watched intently on his computer for the cell phone pings that he had listed, and the three that were showing were Vonni, Nate, and the newcomer Bjoern as he watched the three phones went dead almost at the same exact time, the tower pings showed that the phones went offline, and that was recorded on his computer as a witness to the assassination and that would be the just the proof he needed for payment of the bounty for the hit job that he and his partner had just completed. Julio would submit the data and recordings to the secret dark web that was handling the assignment and the fund's distribution. He would also add the expenses for the endeavor. After the money is sent to his offshore account that would conclude his services for this venture.

Chapter 19

Hanna Torres's Discovery

Hanna Torres was now put in charge of the special dark Ops research team that has been looking at the stolen or unapproved files they have from the Labs that Damek Hava has control of and has been doing top-secret work inside the labs. Like a backroom type of work area but so much bigger and more complex, the work being performed in these labs behind closed doors was being done simultaneously in other labs but at different levels and different procedures with the same goals or outcome in mind. The tests were being done using as many different methods as possible, coming from different approaches. Hanna had the nearly impossible task of finding out what if any that these labs had in common, how they worked in unison, who coordinated all the different tests and how were they documented. Hanna had a large conference room set up with several technicians working on data input. The data would show up on selected jumbo screens on the wall and you could watch the progress of each lab's experiments. Again, these files that they have were retrieved by means that only a Black Ops person could get them by. That was with having their own people inside collecting the data, and as such this data was sometimes several days to over a week old. But it is what it is, and Hanna knew that she would have to fill in the blanks on some of them and wait for the hard file to prove or disprove her thoughts. In almost every case Hanna was spot on. The screens were set up in a random way and wouldn't make a difference but as more and more data came in Hanna with her unique thought pattern started to see something that was abstract at best and in most cases two-dimensional, and in her mind's eye she started to assemble a pattern in the labs' tests. This pattern she saw or sensed was not complete, and she would require a lot more data and study for it to formulate into a working theory. From that, she quite possibly could put together what the labs were doing as a whole, and in essence, a unit is what they were. Hanna was like a pit bull and she sunk her teeth into this project and she tasted blood, and the more she uncovered the more she worked to get the complete picture.

Hanna Torres was sitting in the large display room that has several large computer monitor screens, TV screens actually, and as she sat and watched them the pattern in her mind started to form. She had the ability to move the displays from one to another so in her mind they would make sense. Like reading a book left to right, she configured the screens that had each lab's data running and assembled them to her liking. It was now starting to come together. Some of her technicians could see it as well but not as clearly as Hanna, but what were they seeing? That was the question they all asked. They could see a pattern and system growing. However for this research group, it was like they were assembling a large puzzle with thousands of pieces, and the puzzle pieces were upside down, with no photo fragments just abstract cut shapes. Without the picture of the puzzle, the assembly went slow and the end result was unknown, but Hanna had that intuition that this was big and that it was dangerous.Hanna wanted and needed to know where this was going. Hanna wished she had more data and ultimately she wished she had access to the main computer that each lab was tied to and would drop their data in. Hanna's team would receive thumb drives almost daily from across the world. The flash drives would have, in most cases, duplicate data and overlapping data. The separation, and cataloging of the additional data would take time and the program they had was slow and not exactly set up for the task that Hanna wanted it to perform. This task would need to be done by a human with an inquisitive mind and that was Hanna.

After the data and files were formed into a working theory of sorts, Hanna would go up the ladder and brief them on the progress, the pitfalls, and issues that she has with formulating the end results of these lab experiments and studies.

The labs were working in small sections of their facility on cloning, and each was doing different parts or experiments. When looking at all the work being done at each one it was clear that a lot of small work resulted in a large portion of man hours. At first glance and seeing just the data from one lab it looked benign, but with all the labs in question working on a different segment of the research, the combined time and effort were impressive and elusive to anyone who didn't have access to as much of the data like Hanna Torres has started to put together. This was all preliminary and no real basis for interference from her agency.

Hanna noticed that on the countless files and thumb drives a name was always attached to these files. At least the ones she was interested in or the ones that sent up a red flag and were being researched in multiple labs. The name or reference was to copy or send a copy of the said file to the head of the labs. Even though this person wasn't listed anywhere, as the overseer of them as his name would come up on the ones that caught Hannas' attention. The name was Meir Alter, and Hanna made a note of that name and would do the inquiry and background check, using her black Ops search engine.

Hanna did the background check on Mier Alter and discovered he had passed away. The check found that another group was looking into his family, the group called Knights of Noah, this revelation of their interest sent warning flags up Hanna's spine and now she had no doubt she was on to something. She prepared her brief for her bosses and Hanna had assembled a large file that she would present to them in her effort to escalate the research she and her team was doing. Hanna knew that if she had more resources and better help and of course better data she could get to the bottom of this organization. Hanna presented the files at her next briefing and with the name of Mier Alter tied in with the secret Noah group enticed her superiors to take this to the next level. They informed Hanna what their decision was and that they would add additional field personnel to the project and at this point she was in charge. As usual in government agencies when they have a mission or task at hand they always gave the endeavor a code name and this one was no different. The name on the new mission was called Divine Activity.

Unknown to Hanna, was that her superiors would for the most part disassemble her whole operation and replace it with a smaller more streamlined one, and that they had resources and field people who could retrieve and assemble the data that Hanna wanted and needed. They also had a high-tech computer with an unknown secret program that could and would put all the data in the order that was manageable, and could be read and understood what these labs across the world were up to. They had two individuals in the field they knew were perfect for the job and would work well with Hanna. The Dark Ops group felt this was important enough to draft the retired field agents back into service. The evidence that Hanna had was not only on Cloning but on DNA splicing, virus manipulation, and Gain of Function research. The groups' heads didn't like the secrecy of the research that Hanna discovered and would go full-on board.

Now the Dark Ops group would enlist their people to carry the ball. At this moment their two candidates were undercover and could not be reached as easily as they wanted, so communication with them would go through their handler. Since their handler was offline just now, the project waits for the handler to break protocol or check in at the given time. That didn't sit well with the leaders. They sent the usual coded message out and had to wait until he went from deep silent mode to online as a different person or identity. The group was aware of the mission the handler was on and knew that he would be under wraps for a while, but they also knew that this may be the opportune time to enlist his two charges back into the fold.

Chapter 20

The Jungle

The Cessna 404 landed at an abandoned airfield that was maintained by the Special Black Ops Agency. It was virtually abandoned, but this group has its own sensors at the site to inform the pilots of airspeed and direction so the aircraft could land into the wind. The system was turned on and off by clicking or pulsing the mike 4 times in succession. At that point, the VASI light system would turn on. VASI stands for Visual Approach Slope Indicator, and it would tell the pilot if the bird was too high, on the glide path, or below the glide path. Below was in the jungle, high and you could miss the runway or not have enough room to stop. In any event, these systems plus others would turn on when the mike is keyed in the designated number.

The Cessna 404 landed and came to the end of the runway, turned and taxied to the hidden or camouflaged hanger. When the plane arrived at the hanger a crew of maintenance workers came out of nowhere and positioned themselves around the plane. When the pilot was convinced that all was inline he powered down the engines and made ready for his passenger's departure. The door was opened and the three came out following Padre Juan. As they looked around all they could see was jungle and the sound of many animals and birds. The heat and humidity hit them hard and it was worse than the city they came from. The plane was positioned into the hanger and the large hanger door was closed. The light came on and the group was met by the leader of the support group that was on staff to assist them in every way. This leader went by the name Garcia, and no other name, and that was fine with everyone. Garcia directed the small group to a waiting jungle jeep that would hold them all and their small amount of luggage. He just turned and jumped into the driver seat and proceeded to the destination. Juan was explaining to his now growing group that Garcia was in charge of their protection, that they have to drive up the mountainside to get to the safe house, and that the time involved for the ride could take about an hour. The three, Vonni, Nate, and Bjoern in the mix now started to talk and the noise level of the jeep and the need for secrecy kept the conversation down to a minimum, they arrived at the safe house in just over an hour and the accommodations were what you might say beyond expectations, as it was a large villa on the side of a mountain that could be protected very easily, from all sides. The inside was immaculate, the temperature and humidity was perfect. The three were escorted to their rooms so they could settle in and Juan said he would like to have a meeting in about an hour with just Vonni and Nate to go over their relocation. Juan said he would sit with Bjoern later when he has a plan for him, and that may take some time. Bjoern objected to this and Juan took control and interjected that this is not debatable and that Juan would conference with Bjoern after his meeting with Vonni. Bjoern wasn't thrilled with this but went along, because what could he do in the middle of a jungle mountainside?

Juan sat down in his study and pinged his computer to the satellite, for just a moment to acquire a signal and fast-track any notification from his home base. He immediately received a coded ping that he knew was of utmost importance and that he needed to communicate with the Agency ASAP and the code he received was one that was not used in haste.Juan had never seen it issued before, so he would go through the proper channels to make dark communication with the agency, and the laptop he had would decipher the coded message he received and encrypt the message he sent. Juan received a dossier on Bjoern, and special instruction on the need to enlist Vonni and Nate in the Hanna Torres mission, or what is now called the Divine Activity mission. This enlistment was an order and not a request and Juan was to make it happen at all costs.

The dossier on Bjoern was also sent with special instructions and this new turn of events and orders would take some selling on Juan's part. He's been assigned to put together a team that has almost no experience in this field.Juan's job is to keep the three alive, and complete the mission that the agency wants them to get into.

Juan was able to sit with Vonni and Nate for a brief time and he went over the fact that the two of them were listed as passengers in what appeared to be a fatal aircraft accident. The news stated that the wreckage was at such a remote and dangerous area that only other aircraft could search for survivors and that a land or ground search was not feasible or going to happen. Some because the area doesn't have the equipment, and mostly because the terrain where the wreckage is located is mountainous. So the authorities did an air search and circled the site and took photos, the debris field was large and the parts of the aircraft were unrecognizable. The flights over the crash did not reveal any survivors, they would review each photo over and over to check for any changes or signs of human life and after several days of slow flight aircraft and many photos the search would be called off.

Juan sat down with Bjoern in a private meeting and went over the briefing he had prepared and stated that they were to hold up in this Villa for a short time and that Juan would receive additional orders and instructions on how to proceed from this point in time. Bjoern was still in the dark about why the dark group Noah wanted him so badly. He couldn't understand what was so important in his grandfather's hidden files that would trigger an international secret dark agency to do a worldwide search. The question that Juan asked Bjoern was why, and at that, Juan said that he would need to sit and go over the next course of action in the morning, and that all four of them would attend. Because as Juan put it, this whole mission just got a lot more interesting and difficult, and my next actions will take some planning.Juan excused himself and went back to his study and went to work.

Juan lit up his special government laptop and tied it to the satellite system. The encryption software went to work and the communications between his agency and him started. He received the first of several files and directives and he could see that he had at least 6 more in the queue. He waited until he had all the downloaded files. At that time he would read and go over the orders and extrapolate what he has in a linear sense to produce the best results. If orders are what the agency wants, Juan would make up the methods for how the ends would come together, and in the field, there is nothing as a definite or cut and dried.

The encrypted and decrypted files were set in front of Juan and he knew he had a night of work ahead of him, he would first speed read all the files. After that, he would do the read-and-absorb style of reading. In that mode, he would constantly be working on a plan or mission. The agency had sent their own, and he liked it for the most part, but because he was such good friends with his charges he resisted or refrained from putting them in harm's way. Juan would put together the sales pitch for both Vonni and

Nate and he thought that he could persuade them to come on board with the mission and temporarily come out of retirement. He had the best reasons why. The two were the best for the job and his next hurdle, and it would be the most difficult to get Bjoern in the mix. That sale would take more than Juan had in his bag of tricks, and Juan knew he would need the help and assistance of Vonni and Nate to help convince Bjoern to join their group. Juan knew that the information that he had was so top secret that if any of the recruits didn't want to participate that the final outcome for that person wasn't healthy. Juan could not let them know that part of the equation. Vonni picked up on it right away, but the two men didn't, so Vonni leaned toward joining Juan's group and trying to persuade the others. She would have to do it tactfully so the two men didn't catch on. They would not take kindly to the threat of termination for not joining the newly formed group.

Vonni and Nate were not easy to enlist and the meeting went on for some time. They were the first to be recruited before the task of working on Bjoern, and Juan would need to explain everything from top to bottom to Bjoern. He would hold nothing back and then explain why Bjoern has a role in this mission at all. The explanation and sales pitch went as follows, first Juan would tell all three of them what intel they have and don't have, but where the leads are heading.Juan will show them the documents and brief forms, with the complete files if they want to read them.

The conference Juan had with his new group took all day and they had more questions than Juan had answers. He said he would get them if he could, the meetings that lasted all day were proving to be good for Juan and he still had a lot of convincing. He sent out the questions to his superiors for the questions that the three wanted to be answered, and the meeting would start again when he had the information.

Juan had his whole speech or pitch ready at the beginning of the meeting and he took control on the first day and stated that he would narrate the plan or mission to them in its entirety before he would take questions. The monologue went as follows, from beginning to end.

Chapter 21

Damek Hava And The File BOJ-25:33

During the exploration and research for the secret file that Meir Alter had produced the BOJ-25:33, Damek Hava knew of the secret file, and that any new information would help with finding the formula or procedure that Damek has invested so much time and wealth on. The cure for the blight that has affected his family. The cure was at hand, and just out of reach, or was it in fact just a form of Fata Morgana (mirage)?This was unacceptable for Damek, as he was someone who didn't do well with disappointment or failure. This lost or missing file and now the news of the grandson of Meir Alter in a plane crash in South America, and possibly dying did not hold well with Damek Hava's mood. The death of the grandson of his only true friend Mier was a setback of sorts because Damek thought that the grandson may have information on the missing file. The fact that Bjoern may be dead gave Damek a short feeling of sorrow because he met the man when he was a young lad and could see how smart he was, but not nearly in Miers league, which was a league of its own.

The name of the secret file was now being sought after and an order was given through the labs dark connection to look for anything in their files with a designation or close to the designation of file BOJ-25:33. This order also went out to the Noah Group to include that number in their research.

As this order went out it was picked up by other dark Ops groups in the world and the two groups that this new inquiry would cause a stir in were the Black Ops in the U.S. and the Mossad. No other agencies were looking at any of the data like these two.

The labs started to assemble some data from their archives with the BOJ-25:33 designation listed. The data was incomplete at best, fragmented and coded, and without the key to the code these fragments of coded information could be a recipe for chicken soup. Unlikely as that was, the idea is to put together every bit of information out there in the lab files that are not listed in the mainframe computer with the file number. A tall order to get done and this would not go unnoticed. The flash drives sent into Hanna Torres would show increased activity in searches, and with the order or request for the new file search, the inside dark secret lab workers were tasked with getting more information. Especially about the BOj-25:33 file because this was news to Hanna she was interested in this new piece of the puzzle. The flash drives came in slow but sure and they looked for ways to improve the speed, but safety protocol for the mole agents in the labs was more important.

Damek Hava started to receive an incredible amount of data and information about the coveted file and because most of it was coded and the data coming in was so large Damek would need someone to put the files or data in order and decode the information if they can. Damek put together a small but growing team to work on the fragments and they were all extremely qualified, what Damek was not aware of, was that one of the workers was a dark Ops mole from the U.S. and she was gathering the final information that would be presented to Damek. At the same time, she would send a duplicate copy to her superior Hanna Torres.

The hidden BOJ-25:33 file was not found by Dameks team and the coded fragments they have are proving to be almost unbreakable as to decoding. Meir Alter had his own coding system, and that system would apparently change from time to time almost at its own will, from one page to the next and the meaning of the document would be gibberish. The I.T. people Damek had to work on the decoding were stumped at the complexity of the code. Almost as hard as the German Cipher machine, the Enigma, and this news didn't make Damek any happier. The setbacks, one after the other were getting to him. He cursed the death of his friend Mier, and in the same breath knew the cure was here or close at hand and that thought kept him on track. His team will receive a mountain of documents listed with the files coded BOJ-25:33 or anything close and now they would have to add several large computers to track and organize the massive amounts of data. This whole data storage thing seemed to be more than even a room full of technicians could handle, but Damek didn't care. He wanted, he needed that cure for his family, and he would have it at all costs.

What Damek was not aware of was that almost all of the BOJ-25:33 file data that was out there was either incomplete or obsolete. It was inaccurate and was just the testing that was performed and the results, the massive amount of data that could be found, when assembled would just show the many failed tests, how they were performed, and what procedures were done. Even the file name didn't really give away the true nature of the said file. Because so many different types of tests were being done, almost no one could determine what he was testing or experimenting on. That's because Meir had so many labs doing separate work on the same experiment and listed it as a different test. Virtually the only way to see the big picture was to be inside the mainframe computer and look at each lab separately. At the same time one might put together a large puzzle and as you do the image forms, but to do this, each lab's files would have to be side by side and stacked, and at that, they would have to be configured in a fashion that they made sense. The problems that arise are that the files would have to be opened in a manner that they would coincide with each other. Almost like reading a book from page to page, if you skip a couple of pages the story doesn't make sense. This is what a secret Dark Ops researcher would have to put together just to get a basic handle on the whole picture. No known computer or program written could do that. The task could only be done with a unique abstractly thinking person like Hanna Torres, and she has already put a clear idea and working theory together. The more information she receives the better. However, if she gets any of the coded files she has them stored in a special drive and one that her agency has people working on with their high-tech computers.

The more and more searches and inquiries made in this matter on the dark web, would alert additional players into the fold. Sometimes just as spectators, sometimes the new players or agents of other hostile countries will move people into position to observe. Others wanted to know why they came late to the party and would do whatever, to catch up. This was getting heated on the dark world stage and Damek didn't like that, but he knew the risk was well worth the rewards, and that his families life's depended on this.

Hanna Torres put together another detailed briefing for her superiors and added that they should look at this with urgency. Hanna's thought process was that time was not on their side and the fragments and the assembly of files in the configuration she put them in without a look in the mainframe computer was unbelievably close. The correct assumption that Hanna has is that the labs are working on a new genetic trojan virus that was put in a dormant state, but Hanna's limited amount of intel stopped her short of real hypotheses. Hanna knew from past experience that she would need clear facts and evidence to back up the theory she had. Her superiors also understood that when Hanna had these presumptions they let her run with it because she was usually spot on. So the leaders of her agency added additional funding for the project and informed her of the expanding field personnel, and the streamlining of the project. They let Hanna know that they were trying to incorporate and enlist both Vonni, and Nate to perform the field work for Hanna and that they have another individual who may assist but hasn't been confirmed, Hanna was brought into the higher loop of intel group and her secrecy clearance was changed to make the transition. Hanna was now in the very small dark Ops group of her agency and she would be privy to what is to come next. the agency was onboard with Hanna's doctrine and they had additional intel that leaned the same way that more or less backed up Hanna's briefing.

Hanna would be introduced to Vonni and Nate shortly and they would all work together on this project. What Hanna didn't know was that the third person involved was a relative of the very person that she was investigating. This bit of information may send her in a tailspin. Hanna would need some serious convincing to trust the person that the agency was trying to include in the tight group, but her superiors were sure that they could persuade Hanna to come around. The third player in the field group was none less than Bjoern Jarvia Alter and he wasn't brought on board just yet, so the dream team hasn't been completely assembled at this time.

Chapter 22

The Mountain Jungle Retreat

Padre Juan Guerrero worked all night on the preparation and presentation of his effort to commission and enlist Bjoern into the folds of this new group. The Padre knew that Bjoern may be an intricate part of the mission and Juan would need to use all his powers of persuasion to induce and win over Bjoern. The Padre may need to bring in backup help such as Vonni and Nate if for no other reason than the assurance and trustability that Vonni and Nate have in their handler and the credibility he has. Bjoern would have to make the blind leap and believe this man and go along with the program. Juan knew that it would be a tough sell and just as tough to buy into, so this would take all the powers and tack that Juan has and more. With the proper facts and intel to back his spiel up, Juan has high hopes that he could make it happen. Juan also felt that the mission was time sensitive and of the essence and he would need to get this show on the road sooner than later. He knew that if Bjoern wasn't onboard, he would be detained for an indefinite amount of time while the mission was completed with no loose ends. The meeting that Juan has scheduled would take place just after the next one that he had with both Vonni and Nate. He needed the confirmation that they were indeed onboard and at that point Juan would move on to Bjoern.

The meeting Juan had with Vonni and Nate went on and lasted for several hours and Juan went into details about what was expected of them. He said that the world was told that the two of them went down in a plane crash in South America that there were no survivors and that on the aircraft was another unknown passenger that perished as well and that the identity of this passenger was not known for now.

Juan went on to explain the situation in the States and what the agency had uncovered so far, was that a single person, (Damek) and his family were working on a cure that had plagued this particular family for a long time. That this so-called plague was just coming to light over the last hundred years maybe more, but was felt by the family about that time. That this plague if it is one, was getting worse for this group and this group or family was very large and had thousands in it across the world, all with different degrees of this sickness.

The Agency has come across intel that has shown that this extremely large and influential family has been working on the cure and has control of many labs and pharmaceutical companies across the Globe and that these labs have been secretly working on this very selective plague that the Damek group have and from what the intel shows they have found the cure. However, the cure as it were, is missing and this elite group has been franticly searching for the file and so far has come up dry. Juan showed both Vonni and Nate what Hanna Torres has found to date, and her findings and theory. Juan has a copy of the briefing and facts that back up Hanna's preliminary findings, and Hanna and the Agency have high confidence that her theory is correct. However, to prove the hypothesis Hanna needs more data and if possible a look into the main computer that houses all the different lab's experiments. The labs across the world are connected to one main computer and no one knows about this mainframe unit but the owner and founder Damek Hava.

The scourge or curse that has ravaged the Damek Hava family is a slow death from what is called mutagenesis,(the occurrence or induction of mutation in DNA) and the Damek people have a particular form of this disease, that is only evident in the Damek family. Damek has been working on the cure for as long as labs and pharmaceutical companies have been in business, and now a cure has been found and is lost or missing.

Mutagenesis disease, if you could call it a disease, is the process by which an organism's DNA changes resulting in gene mutations. The mutation was thought to be a permanent and heritable change in genetics. That is true in almost all cases, but not the Dameks Family, because they as a unit are unique and have the DNA that can recover from the curse if this mutation was identified in some way and a cure was made. It seems that a very active and overzealous, scientist, and mathematician, that has worked on this Dilemma for well over 75 years has come up with a countermeasure to reverse the dreaded Mutagenesis disease. However, the process that needs to take place may not be in the best interest of others and Hanna Torres brief states that the cure to save the thousands and thousands of the Dameks Hava family may require countless other humans to forfeit their lives. The exact number is unknown at this time, mostly because it's unknown how many family members are in the Damek group, and that number would give a better or maybe an exact amount of causalities. From what the agency knows or thinks they know from the pilfered flash drives that Hanna has systematically put in order has shown that the numbers could be astronomical.

After the briefing, Juan had with Vonni and Nate, about this new world crisis as it is, or maybe, the three took a short break and Juan said he would come back and explain in more detail what he and the Agency's expectations or participation were from them. Juan left the two and went to work on the next phase of the mission which was to entice and convince Bjoern to come on board and join the mission, not only to join but to be fully vested in the cause, Juan needed the three to work as a team. The fact that Vonni and Nate didn't know the connection between Bjoern and the mission just yet would make the effort more difficult. Juan knew or thought he could make the deal, and they would go along with the program. The next part of convincing Bjoern would be difficult at best, and would take every bit of Juan's skills of getting people to comply with what he wanted them to.

First things first, Juan needed his two charges in the mission and at that time he would spell out their parts and how the mission would progress. After, both Vonni and Nate would take the reins and run with the ball, only to make reports to Juan when they have results and what the daily plans are so that Juan could put security and protection in place.

Juan sat back down with Vonni and Nate and finalized their involvement in the mission. They were fully invested and agreed to do the mission.At that time Juan explained the inherent dilemma the mission has, and what they had to overcome. That was that their friend Bjoern was possibly involved in the mission because Bjoern was the grandson of the scientist who worked for the Damek Hava family. This tidbit of new information stunned both Vonni and Nate and now they had to know how deep this new factor was and whether was Bjoern even aware of the scheme that his grandfather was involved in. Juan informed the two that his intel showed that Bjoern was not and had no knowledge of what his grandfather was doing or involved in, but Juan felt that Bjoern may have some information or access to some. In any event, Juan's thought process was that the mission could use Bjoern and his name to open some doors to places that would be difficult for his Agency to get into. So Juan explained to Vonni and Nate the importance of securing Bjoern into the team and they agreed.

The next hurdle was to sit down and enlist Bjoern into the team, and this would prove to be more difficult than first thought, some because Bjoern loved his grandfather and didn't want to tarnish his name in any way, and second Bjoern didn't exactly trust Juan yet. That was another barrier to get over, so the next phase of this convincing would take longer than Juan thought. And again, time is of the essence, and the kicker is that if Bjoern refused to join the mission he would not be allowed to leave the mountain villa, until this escapade was over.Because Bjoern now knew of Juan and the dark Ops he may not be given the life he had before his trip. These dark Ops agents knew their jobs and the mere fact that Bjoern was listed as the other passenger on the downed plane that was never recovered could make his disappearance that much easier. Juan would never make that threat, but that was an option and the Agency looked at all options. Juan wanted Bjoern with them because the success of the mission would increase with him rather than without him, so taking the extra time to convince Bjoern was worth it.

Chapter 23

Bjoern Connection

The briefing and meeting went poorly between Bjoern, and Juan, and he used his best tact with him. Because of the distrust and the actual location of the Villa and everything that had occurred to this point, made Bjoern more irate, and given his lawyer instinct and sharp mind he would look at, and analyze everything that Juan said. He would look for holes in every statement and ask questions that Juan may not have liked but would answer to keep the dialogue going. So this meeting of the minds proved more difficult than Juan anticipated and more challenging. But Juan wasn't a quitter and knew the importance of having Bjoern with the team, Juan went over the facts as he had them and that Juan thought that the team would work well together. But again Bjoern was reluctant to join and stated he wanted additional intel and time to digest what he had to make a decision. So the meeting went on and more and more intel was shared and Juan would give everything he could to Bjoern short of a security breach.Juan explained the importance of Bjoern's participation. He went over the exact same document that he had gone over with Vonni and Nate and he explained to Bjoern that his two friends were indeed on board. At some point, Bjoern was starting to soften and get slightly persuaded to at least hear the whole story with an open mind.When Juan saw that Bjoern had made the turn to being receptive he called for a break, and at that point Juan would ask for a meeting of all of the group.Juan scheduled the sit down for later that day, and stated he would have additional information for Bjoern to see, in hopes that the trust factor between him and Bjoern can get resolved.

Later that day the second scheduled meeting was held with all the participants and at this time Juan said to the group that he would have to reveal the true nature of Vonni, Nate, and Juan's relationship. He looked at both Vonni and Nate and received the nod that they were okay with it. At that point, Juan started with the proverbial history and summary of the story behind Vonni and Nate.Juan went on and gave the short version of the story that got directly to the point and Juan would leave the floor open for Q&A after his tales of the recent past.

The story that Juan told Bjoern went something like this; the reason why Vonni, Nate, and I are so close and entwined, is because I'm what is called their handler. But I'm much more. I protect them from danger of every kind and the reason why they require my services is that in the not-so-distant past both of them did a service for their country and the world and I'll go into that in a minute. They were relocated under what is called World Witness Protection and this system is funded by the U.N.The agency that runs and administers the system is so top secret that it's virtually impossible to access or hack, and the people that run it at the top are incorruptible and just short of pure at least in Juans views.

Juan went on and explained that the next part he was about to reveal would put Bjoern and the rest of them in peril of the worst kind and that Juan has the okay from his superiors and from both Vonni and Nate to include you in the so-called team. Juan said

'I'm slightly reluctant to move forward with the next part", however, I think that we need you as part of the team as does everyone else. With that being said let me go into the reason why my two friends are in the WWPP, or World Witness Protection Program.

Juan started the history lesson or story by saying, remember a few years ago when the world was on the brink of a world war and Israel was surrounded by so many other countries, and their destruction was imminent. No one knew how it was led to that stage, and when the war started and ended so quickly and the dust settled. A new mandate was put in place for world peace and that all three religions would be taught at the same time in the countries that had conflicts like Islam, Judaism, and Christianity. The U.N. was revamped and changed for the better.Bjoern said he remembers that time frame very well and that's when Juan informed Bjoern that the plot to destroy the world system and make a one-world order was subjugated by none other than Vonni and Nate, and that at the time they went by Yvonne and Johnathon. They had another player who was instrumental in their success, Yossele Schumacher, and Juan didn't go into what Yossele did for a living or that he was Mossad.

Juan explained how the three of them, Yvonne, Johnathon, and Yossele went about getting the intel and stopping the one world-order movement that was almost unstoppable. In a near Doomsday scenario, Juan was telling this story to Bjoern so he would understand the connection and trust that he and his charges have and that Juan wants to have with Bjoern. After the history lesson, Juan said so whether you are fully onboard at this time or not I'm going to explain the next phase of our mission with hopes that you will join and participate.

Juan started with what they have so far, the briefing that he has from Hanna Torres, where they want to go, and why Juan thinks that Bjoern is so important to the undertaking. The story that Juan told was exactly what he told Vonni and Nate. That the many labs around the world were working on a secret cure for a special group of people or family, and that from what they have at this point was inconclusive but damming. That's where Yvonne and Johnathon, and now Bjoern come in. The Agency or Black Ops wants the three of them to go on a mission to uncover what exactly these labs are doing and what the cure is which seems to be the single most important file that the Damek and Noah group is looking for.

Juan also stated that time was of the essence and that all hands needed to be on deck, or at least we needed to know who was our teammate. At that point, both Vonni and Nate turned to Bjoern and as they sat in their chairs close together almost huddled up Bjoern looked deeply into his friend's eyes. He trusted them with his life, and he could see that they trusted their lives with Juan and that the two considered Juan as a personal friend. The two gave Bjoern the look that friends give to accept another in the click, and Bjoern went from not trusting Juan to semi-trusting to total trusting in one afternoon. But Bjoern was still at odds with going after the data and investigating his grandfather. That Bjoern resisted, but relented when he read and heard more and more intel. Bjoern would concur and he came onboard without reservations.

After the meeting the four took a break and had some wine and other snacks and they resumed the conversation and how they would proceed, as they sat around the bistro-type table in the mountain Villa looking out at the view and going over the last couple of hours of conversation, Bjoern and Vonni were talking and Nate was listening to both and paying attention to Juan going back and forth. That's when Vonni asked Bjoern the question, that has not been asked to this date, and that was why Bjoern was down here in South America and why the impromptu visit. She said she remembered that Bjoern said he had something he wanted to show her, but that seemed like a lifetime ago. That's when Bjoern said oh ya he forgot that he has a flash drive with him that he wants Vonni to look at, and Vonni said you came all the way down here to show me a flash drive? That's odd.

Both Juan and Nate picked up on what Bjoern had just said, and it piqued their interest as well, and everyone became quiet waiting for the explanation, and that's when Bjoern began his story.

Chapter 24

The Flash Drive Decoding

Bjöern would explain in brief how after his grandfather passed he received many pieces of property. When Bjoern received the contents of the wills package it had several key rings that were for the rental units that his grandfather had. Bjoern explained that he did an inventory of the rentals and found one that wasn't rented with specific orders and that it should never be rented. So Bjoern would go to this property to view it, and it was a large home and he had a cluster of keys that went with this house. He didn't know why this would be, so many keys for one house. Bjoern did his investigation and found the file that his grandfather left him to read that Bjoern thought was over the top and interesting and now it's starting to make sense. Bjoern also explained what he found hidden in the wall of the basement, a hidden or concealed part of the house that would require the keys that he has on the large key ring to open. With that revelation, Juan almost came out of his shoes, but was a professional and contained himself. No one in the room could see or feel that Juan's anxiety just spiked. Juan felt that he may have found the Holy Grail, or Mother Load as some may refer to it. Juan knew he would have to tread slowly and cautiously. Some because Bjoern wasn't one hundred percent happy about giving up his grandfather's secrets, and possibly making him look bad. Bjoern wanted to keep Mier Alter's name in good standing with no black marks. Juan interjected again that his goal was not to destroy his grandfather's legacy but to find out what was going on in the secret labs.

Juan also made it clear that he thought that Meir Alter was working on a cure and certainly wasn't involved in what his Agency thought the final solution came to. Juan stated that his thoughts are that possibly, when Meir found out what the cure was and would do he hid it from his best friend Damek Hava in an effort to see if there was another way to proceed. Juan also stated that they just have theories and nothing solid, and that's where Bjoern and this team come in. They as a team will research and investigate everything they can find. Juan said finally that this whole mission may be a bust, but we need to go where the evidence takes us. With those sacred words and the assurances from his good friends Vonni and Nate, he made the leap and became a full partner. As the intel would come in Bjoern would be more vested, and involved.

Bjoern decided to share his flash drive with his new group, the Divine Activity Union. Vonni looked at it and said, ok let's get to work. She inserted the drive into her laptop. The files that appeared were all coded and her computer couldn't decipher the files. She was a bit dismayed at the revelation and looked at Bjoern and said what is this? He said that's the problem, almost all the files that are hidden in the rental basement are coded like that or very much like it. That's why I'm here, and that's the problem I have. All three of the new team members watched as the files scrolled through each one and saw that the drive had an incredible amount of information. They were all at their wit's end as to what they could or would do next. The whole time Juan was sitting in the background and observing the team and watching how they worked together. Juan needed to see how they would react and how they would respond to a roadblock. They started to brainstorm on how they would crack the code and they all had different ideas and plans. They worked as a team would, that had been together for years and that's exactly what Juan wanted to see. He was pleased with the way the mission was starting. After Juan had been satisfied with what he saw he stepped in and took control as a handler would, and informed the threesome that the state department had given him a special laptop for this mission. It was unique and one of a kind and he explained to Vonni that this laptop was better and more powerful and hi-tech than the QCA computer she had during her last mission. The name or designation for this particular laptop and its software is called Asgardians 777. It has been under development for years and has recently been perfected to the point that this software is well into the ninety percentile range of cracking and deciphering codes. This system was tried on the WW2 German enigma machine and was extremely successful. However, the Asgardians 777 took several hours of collaborative learning, and that part of the software learns from each other by working together to solve a problem, complete a task, and create a product, such as the final deciphered code. This software, the Asgardians 777 never stops working as it goes on to the next code or document. The system does what may be referred to as block learning, because it adjusts its own system or the way it decoded that last document with any new information the software has evolved into. With the newly updated learning the software has done, the fastest GPU clock speed in the non-military world is 3.45 GHz. This secret quad core 3 terabyte memory computers clock speed is well over 10.5 GHz. The computer will go back and redo the last set of documents and make it more accurate, and try to achieve the famous one hundred percent accuracy, and that is unachievable. Coding has been around since mankind has been scribing, from Hieroglyphic writing to Sumerian and Cuneiform writing of the Near East, decipherment by the Asgardians 777 on these writings has been very successful. However, the results of the findings have been kept secret for fear that foreign actors may get wind of the power and existence of the Asgardians 777. The machine has the power to decode any code given the required amount of time. The updates continue to improve its speeds. As of now, the Asgardians 777 can decode almost any document within hours, and if the system has done the same kind of decoding before, the time frame drops down considerably.———

—

Juan explained the laptop to Vonni, Nate, and Bjoern and stated that this was a top-secret, that no one outside this room knew about its existence other than the State Department and his Black Ops agency, and that a breach of that secrecy could mean death or imprisonment. Juan asked if the three understood and if it was clear what he had just said, and they all said it was crystal clear.

Juan went on to explain that the mission was to get to the bottom of the lab experiments and what they were doing. That they as a group may be put in a dangerous position, but that may or may not be the case. They all were prepared to move forward and at that, Juan said ok let's get cracking and put that flash drive into the 777. As soon as they did that, the laptop started to work and it showed that the estimated time to decipher would be between six and ten hours. Mostly because the 777 has never seen this coding before and will need to make a centerline, or start point and work outward. Once the 777 has some of the coding completed, the software will learn and become more proficient. As it does the time to decipher drops down and the accuracy goes up. At this point, there wasn't anything else the group could do. They broke for the day and the three new mission partners decided to go to the study and talk about the last chain of events.Juan begged off from the conversation stating that he had a lot of other mission planning to perform.

Juan went to his private study to get in touch with his superiors and brief them on the day's progress and that he would send an encrypted document with his full analysis of the mission's success or failure. He informed the Agency that he was in possession of a coded flash drive and the 777 was working on it. He went on to explain the possible importance of this said drive. Juan worked on different scenarios and different mission plannings that may come up. Juan was not the type to get caught flat-footed and he almost always had a contingency plan or what some would call plan b-c-d. Juan researched the way that Vonni and Nate accomplished the last mission they were on, and he read the brief. Then he read the complete file and he found that they had a special co-partner that was instrumental in their success on the last mission. An individual who absolutely kept them alive and did the dirty work that Vonni and Nate were unaware of. This co-partner was well connected on the European Stage at the time and from what the file says was Mossad. That tidbit of information intrigued Juan so he dug deeper into this other player and found that the third person who was in Vonni'e group during the last mission was a Mossad agent and has since retired. Juan knew that was bull, as agents from the Mossad never really retire. They may go on reserve and be called up at any time, this other member was now a professor working at a University in Israel that the students all called prof Shume. This professor was okay with the nickname. Juan did his research on his Agency's Dark Web, on Professor Shume, and found that the professor wasn't as retired as he said he was. He still had his hand in the proverbial spy game at all times. His research also found that Prof. Shume was at this very moment in South America. This bit of information caught Juan off guard, but he liked the thought that there was another player in the area that was a friend and not an enemy. So Juan sent out his message to his people to quietly and covertly look for and observe this Professor and report back to him.

Juan started making plans for the trip back to the States via private lear Jet so his group and the 777 computer could look at the hidden files that Bjoern had spoken of. The group would have new identities and passports and would come into the country through a secret military base so they wouldn't have the problem of going through customs and having issues. Juan had made the request that the rental house be watched from a distance and that maybe another house in the immediate area get rented by his backup agents to secure that house for his team when they arrived. The 777 was working on the flash drive and Juan was completing his tasks and putting the mission together. Juan would need to speak to Vonni and Nate about Professor Shume. Juan had mixed feelings about this man and needed some additional inside info from these two.

Chapter 25

BOJ-25:33 File

Damek Hava was still frantically looking for the BOJ-25:33 file that had the cure.

So far all he has are fragments of it and the promise of more to come from his private researchers, who seemed to believe they were on the threshold of finding additional files. They had high hopes that the BOJ-25:33 was part of the cache they are procuring soon. This made Damek relax a bit but he was still hyper. Again, this was not his normal self of always being in control. He was in uncharted waters for this emotion.

The research group Knights of Noah were the very best at what they do, and left no stone unturned. This group was accessing every lab house computer for the information they searched for. What the Noah group didn't know was that these house computers were tied into, and did an information dump into another main frame that was offsite. The mainframe was so well protected with firewalls. The way this one works is it allows data to enter another computer and then it scans that data. That data gets sent to another computer and the process gets done again, like washing or scrubbing the data for any viruses. Going through this process it's virtually impossible to access the mainframe files. That would have to be done with a manual connection and then any files could be copied from hands-on, or looked at via screens. The memory of this mainframe computer is measured in several Exabytes or (EB). One EB is 1000

Petabytes or one billion gigabytes (GB). That's an enormous amount of storage and memory, and may be the largest in civilian control. Access to this mainframe and its secrets would take years to read, understand, and apply. Of course, the files in this unique secret computer are encrypted by none other than Meir Alter himself. That would prove to be a problem. The Noah group found fragments of the BOJ-25:33 file. This group had its own specialist that could look at data and files and assemble them to make sense, and in an orderly fashion. Since Damek allowed this research group access, they pulled up an incredible amount of files and were in the process of assembling the data into the final product or the BOJ-25:33 file. This file would show Damek how to make the cure, and what the side effects or collateral damage were. The data that was received at this point was promising and the Noah group felt they would complete the task at hand very soon. However, they also knew they would need additional data. They knew what they had was not complete. This group relayed this bit of information to Damek. Even though he wasn't pleased with that revelation, he was happy with the progress the group had made so far, and he had high hopes that his coveted cure would be his soon.

BOJ-25:33 file in its entirety was in Meir Alters's hidden rooms in the rental house, and the file was coded.Meir was certain when he wrote the encryption that it was impossible to crack without the key. He was confident that even with the key the coded file wouldn't be opened, because the key to open the encryption was coded in a way that only he understood just by looking at the key, which looked like α̣ Ω̣ +,- 1111+(0,1,1,2,3,5,8,13,21,34,55,89,144,233)#+-%~*. This particular sequence of numeric and Greek letters is on each file, and repeated throughout the file at the bottom of the file itself. Meir could look at the key that was listed at the bottom of the page and instantly be able to decode the file that was written in the multiple shorthand scribe, and in whatever language he was writing the shorthand in. Meir was fluent in several foreign languages, so even with the key the decoding became more difficult for anyone else because of the multi-shorthand styles that they were coded in. This particular encryption would use whatever language and whatever mathematics that Meir thought would keep his file unreadable to anyone but himself. He was well-versed in the scribe of the ancient Sumerian writing and cuneiform script, which was developed well before and predating the Egyptians. In any event, only a select few people on the planet could read and understand the Sumerian writing. Damek was also fluent in it, but no computer known could decode the file without the specific code key and knowledge of these ancient people and their alphabet. The computer, to do all that would need to be almost as large as a supercomputer or one that requires a large building to house it in. However, one did exist, and it was in the possession of a newly formed special group that had been given the secret code name of Gilgamesh. A sub-group working with Hanna Torres's mission, designation Divine Activity, and the newly formed company armed with this Asgardians 777 Decryption software system. They will be en route back to the States, just as soon as the 777 breaks the coded flash drive.

The next thing on Damek's long list of affairs to complete was to communicate quietly with his very large family that the cure was at hand. They should get prepared, and get their affairs in order. His family all knew what that meant, and what their next procedure should be when they receive the next communique, and they all would be ready.

Damek had at least ninety percent of the BOJ-25:33 file in his possession, however, the data wasn't in the correct indexes, and that would take some time to put together. The Noah group assured him that another large fragmented file was on its way, and that the Noah group was still searching for anything else out there.

Damek would have his own newly acquired pharmaceutical, and biochemist start working on the large BOJ-25:33 file he has. To make it readable and functional, Damek knew would be difficult because the files were incomplete. That made the process of putting the final draft in the correct order virtually impossible. But Damek wanted his new man to get familiar with what they had so far. To start the process and do what he can. Even though they both knew it was futile, and maybe counter-productive. But Damek wanted some movement on this and he always got what he wanted, so his new man Friedrich started working on the file. He could see it was a cure for some disease but that some parts were missing, and that the semblance of the file was not going to be accurate or perfect.Fredrich didn't like that at all and he let Damek know his feelings. However, he had to do it VIA encrypted emails, because no one other than Meir and Dameks family and Bjoern when he was a young boy had ever seen Damek in person, or knew that Damek was Damek, as he was a ghost to all and never seen.

Chapter 26

Asgardians 777

The 777 finished working on the flash drive and the brief that came out to show how accurate the decoding was. The 777 showed that it was only at about 72 percent accurate, but will show and brief what it has.Juan was disappointed at the 72 percent accuracy. But he knew that over time as the block learn kicks in, and the 777 gets more and more data, to decode this will get better and the percentages will increase.Juan also knew that as time went on the 777 would go back and rework this file and increase the accuracy as its software learns. This is a process and it will take time and a lot more coded information.

The flash drive brief showed that what it has is a long list of successful and failed tests on thousands of different viruses. The tests were on how these viruses reacted to different stimuli and how they faired under different conditions, and different blood types. Most of the tests that were done were done for many years. They were old and outdated. But what was different was that these tests were being done a bit differently. They were being performed with subjects of different ages and blood types, and many different heritages. However, with an accuracy at the 72 percentile, it's not the best marker for what these labs were trying to accomplish. With this limited new data, Juan sent this to his researcher Hanna Torres, with a warning that what he's sending is not perfect, and she should take it at face value or the 72 percent accuracy. The good news was that even as difficult as the code was, it was somewhat deciphered, and to Juan, that was a win, and he was taking that well.

Juan sat down with his new group and went over the flash drive and the 777 briefings and the accuracy. Juan explained that the code that Meir had made was extremely difficult and that the 72 percent was outstanding. He went on to say that as the 777 decoded more data it would learn and get better. the 777 would submit another brief for the team. Juan informed the team that they would start the mission tomorrow, but that he had one loose end to work out. He hoped to clear that up within the next hour. When that was complete, he would sit down with them again and make the game plan.

Juan went back to his study and sent a message to his superiors via encrypted satellite asking if he could include Professor Shume in the group. If the Prof had passed the background check, and if they received the okay from the Professors people to include him. The transmission and request would take some time so he would need to wait for a response. In the meantime, Juan would start the preparation for the insertion of his new Gilgamesh group. He would need new identities and passports and the whole black Ops style of doing business.This part was going to be the easiest part of his mission, Juan made the plan B to include the professor if he was now a member and Juan also had plan A without him. The plan would be more or less to get set up in the Chicago area, get into the rental house, copy every file they could find, and let the 777 go to work. Juans' second part of the mission was to involve the Gilgamesh group in Hanna Torre's world. That was a tall order, because no one outside the agency was allowed in, so they would need special clearance. After that Juan would have to work on Hanna to accept the Gilgamesh members as part of this mission. From his past experience with his agency, and especially

Hanna this would be the next big hurdle and they had to get past it one way or the other if the agency wanted the mission to succeed.Hanna Torres was and is an exceptional lady and probably the smartest that Juan had ever met. Outside of work, she was a super nice person. But when it came to her work and her division she was overprotective, and almost never let anyone inside her little circle of trust let alone her Black Ops world. Juan would use all his powers to make this happen. He thought that if Hanna could see the value in the Gilgamesh group and that they were, let's say her team, maybe she could let them in, and she would collaborate and cooperate with them. This would take time, and that's not something they had, at least from what Juan was seeing in his secret intel files, and he was seldom wrong.

Juan received confirmation to include Professor Shume in the Gilgamesh team. He was informed that the Professor was apprized on his end, that he was now out on loan, and would share all intel he felt was safe with them. The Professor was updated with all the member's background files. He knew who he was working with. The Professor didn't know who Bjoern was, but was pleased to see that he would be working with his old friends Vonni and Nate.Although he was aware of Juan and his reputation the Professor knew little about him. The dark file he received showed less than he expected, and that bothered the Professor. But he has gotten over bigger obstacles, and he was assured that this Gilgamesh team and Juan were safe. Since his two friends from the past were members he felt better about it. After he made contact with Juan the usual way through a phone line and the two talked in dark Ops code that just they understood, and Juan got the jist of the conversation that the Professor was all in. He would meet up with them ASAP. Juan said he was not sure when that would be, but he would stay in close contact and he would let his guests know that they may have a visitor in the near future for dinner. The Professor understood that the Gilgamesh team were getting ready to move out.

Juan sat back in his chair and closed his eyes for a moment. He couldn't remember when he had more than a couple of hours of sleep at one time, and although he was used to that, he was tired. His next job was sitting with his team and bringing them up to speed as to when they will depart, and how Juan had planned the mission. As he was explaining everything to his people and they were all on board, he dropped the Professor bomb on them, and let them know that we have another member in the team. Juan just said they recruited a Professor into the team and left off his name.He waited for the group to react to the news. At first, they were stunned, then maybe felt betrayed and then they started to argue a bit. They said they feel they have a good team and don't need any outsiders. Vonni, Nate, and Bjoern agreed on this, and that's when Juan told the group the Professor's full name, Yossele Schumacher. Both Vonni and Nate's eyes lit up and they were almost giddy. Bjoern looked at the two of them and asked what was going on, and the two explained their past with Yossele and that he had more or less kept them alive. They trusted him wholeheartedly, and they hoped that Bjoern would accept him into the circle.Bjoern thought about it for a while and said I'll have an open mind on it. He said, Vonni if you say this man is okay, then that's good enough for me, but give me some time to process it and get to know him. They all agreed to welcome a new warrior in.

Juan was pleased with the setting and he had everything moving forward. He informed the Gilgamesh group that they would be departing for the States tomorrow and to pack whatever they had. Which wasn't that much, so Juan took the liberty of getting a lot of luggage and miscellaneous items so customs wouldn't look at them funny. Their first stop in the States after settling into a hotel would be to meet up with Hanna Torres. That could prove to be a day to remember for all parties. But Juan would take several hours to work on Hanna to help the progression move smoothly, and to reassure Hanna that she was the Lead on this unless someone from above said differently.Juan let Hanna know that he was at her beck and call. Once Hanna had that assurance from Juan, she would work with the Gilgamesh group more freely, and this would make Juan's job a lot easier. After that, Juan had to break the news to Hanna that Yossele Schumacher was also a part of the team. That set her off, because she didn't trust the Mossad and she knew of Yossele and his past. But Hanna didn't have any bad intel on him or anything that she didn't like so she said she was okay with him, but would be watching him very closely. These Black Ops people just look at each other a different way than the rest of us. I guess they can see themselves in each other.

Chapter 27

Assembly Of The Infamous File

Friedrich the new scientist who worked for Damek was now getting additional files that had the BOJ-25:33 designation in them. Friedrich had to research through the multitude of files and ascertain what if any of this new information was relevant or had a direct bearing on the special file. He was making progress, slow as it is. Friedrich knew that he would need a lot more information to bring about a finished product. He also knew he was on the right track from what he had. It showed that the cure would need additional data for him to complete the file and procedure. Fredrich has set up his research area in a large abandoned-looking warehouse. However, this building was quite the opposite, the inside was state-of-the-art, and had all the trappings of good a/c and lighting and set up very much like an office complex would be.Fredrich had his crew, or team working on the fragmented files and putting them in their computer that was set up specifically for lab, math, and experimental work. This undertaking that was laid upon Fredrich was daunting, to say the least, and almost overwhelming. To most, it would be, but Fredrich was exceptional and he would keep going. Fredrich was starting to buy into this whole concept as he sees it so far, and feels that this cure could save millions of lives. He was getting drawn into what Damek wanted.

The file was getting assembled as quickly as could be expected. From what Fredrich could see so far, to his amazement a lot of the experiments were performed on human patients from all walks of life, and all ages. Although this caught him off guard, Fredrich's thought process and belief was that the needs of the many always outweighed the needs of the uncommon or occasional test subject. He could see that these test subjects were used in virus testing and cures. What he didn't understand, was that the test was successful. The same subjects would then be given another virus after the last one went dormant. And then another and another. These viruses that were administered were some that were from another time. They were what is called the inherited viruses, or the ones that are part of the DNA of the test subject. These particular viruses are by any other term benign, because they are part of the human make-up and have been with us for thousands of years. In essence these viruses from thousands of years ago have integrated their DNA into ours and they are harmless. So why were these ancient viruses isolated and reintroduced into the subjects, and then given the cure for the particular virus? This whole process didn't make sense. Some of the test people were given so many different viruses and cured they seem to be almost immune to almost any out there. Also, every one of them went dormant just like the virus Chickenpox does after the vaccine, it goes dormant.

Fredrich found in another batch of documents that the actual cure they were looking for involved damage to a person's DNA and that startled Fredrich and confused him because he knew of no cure or procedure that could reverse DNA damage. He was even more interested in the cure. Because if there is a cure, or fix to help the many with this affliction he was all for the tests.Fredrich just didn't see any correlation between the virus testing that was so extensive and this hidden cure that was yet to come. But Fredrich liked what he saw and he was amazed at the progress that Meir Alter had made.

Fredrich is a direct descendant of the infamous German Heydrich, from WWII. Although Fredrich changed his last name to Becker, Damek knew his history and knew what was in Fredrich's heart, and the apple doesn't fall far from the tree.

Fredrich was curious why the test subjects had so many tests done, one after the other. His question was who would subject themselves to that kind of abuse or exploitation? It finally occurred to him that the subjects that were getting tested may not have had a choice, and that made sense. This opened the door to the thought of possible human trafficking, for medical testing. That consideration hadn't entered Fredrich's mind until this moment. He would keep that tidbit of information locked in his thoughts for a later date. What Fredrich was trying to get to the bottom of was how a cure to repair damaged DNA, and what if any, the testing of the many viruses had in the cure. He couldn't make the connection, although he was confident that he would soon. Especially with the massive amounts of data coming in. Fredrich's job was cut out for him, but the puzzle was starting to come together as such, and he was getting excited. During this assembly of the file, Fredrich was studying and learning as much as he could find, on damaged DNA cures and viruses. He found that Ancient Viral DNA plays a role in Human Disease and Development, and that the remnants of ancient viral pandemics in the form of viral DNA sequences embedded in the genomes are still active in healthy people. This makes up around eight percent of the human genome, left behind as a result of infections that humanity's primate ancestors suffered many many years ago. They became part of the human genome due to how they replicate. So with this new information that Fredrich has learned he can see a small window of possibility that a damaged DNA cure can be made.

But Fredrich was definitely out of his league on the concept. He would have to ask his boss, Damek if he could confer with another professional. One that Fredrich has full trust and feels could be trusted but would be needed to complete the project at hand.

Damek was on board with a professional DNA BioStatus Analysis and researcher, for a quicker resolution to the final solution. Fredrich had a friend that he grew up with from Germany who was very good and was known for their not-so-legal experiments. This person's name is Frieda Von Helm. She was accused of doing illegal human cloning, and may still be doing the experiments to this day. For Frieda Von Helm to work with Fredrich he would have to seduce her into the research he was doing, with the promise that she may be able to continue her vocation and work in the Pluripotent stem cell induction field,(human cloning) and she agreed.Damek's secret mission was coming together and getting closer, the BOJ-25:33 data was getting sorted and incorporated into a workable file and there was a lot more work to perform, but the progress was picking up speed and the light at the end of the tunnel was dim but still it was there.A few weeks ago there was no light at all, so for that, Fredrich was getting anxious and his mood was changing. With his new assistant Frieda, he could move the needle faster and he was happy with that. Fredrich now had someone he could bounce his thoughts and questions off of. He could take questions from Frieda and they as a team would tackle and solve the perplexing and laborious job ahead of them. But now they had a better chance at a positive result.

Chapter 28

Gilgamesh and Asgardians 777

The Secret newly formed group called the Gilgamesh team was preparing to leave for their destination and fly back to the States. Before they could, Juan would need to assemble the group with the newest member Yossele Schumacher, so they could get to know each other and for Bjoern to accept Yossele into the group. Before they started the journey and a new mission, Bjoern's acceptance of Yossele wasn't a deal breaker. But Juan would like his team all pulling and working together in unison. It would work for much better results and a lot quicker. Juan didn't want to be a babysitter, and have to keep the peace. The best scenario was they all work together for the greater good.

The plane that Juan sent to pick up Yossele at his airport was a six-seater prop job, and Yossele had some of his people with him, as that's a standard operating procedure. No Mossad agent was sent out into the field without a backup, or shadow and this was no different. Yossele's people consisted of a 4 person backup. This group was trimmed down to only two besides Yossele. One was a young lady who was extremely good at her job, the other was a young male agent. They both had several years in the Mossad, and had many assignments that went very well. Yossele was at ease with these agents and felt he was in good hands. When they landed in the Jungle near Juans villa the two Mossad agents would do their thing and just blend in the background as they were not part of the Gilgamesh mission team. They were for security and the safety of Yossele and they could and would do several other jobs as needed. But at this point, they would just shadow Yossele and stay in the background.

The meeting went as expected with all team members. The obstacle that had to be crossed was the Bjoern and Yossele personality acceptance. Juan had cocktails set up for the group with all the usual drinks and Hors d'oeuvres and they sat around. Juan moved the conversation to a neutral place so that these two men could find common ground. That wasn't easy because of the obvious differences, but what they both had in common was their friendship and admiration for Vonni, and that was the icebreaker. So Juan steered the conversation around Vonni's career in South America and how she has been doing and how her law office was doing.That brought Bjoern into the conversation because he was an attorney and they both loved the law. Sometimes the two didn't agree on it and would debate it. Yossele was no slouch in the legal business both foreign and domestic, and could keep up with the two. The debates and conversations would start and continue and resolve at its own volition. This was Juan's way of getting everyone talking and getting to know each other and each other's passions. After dinner they would have additional drinks and the lawyer talk would resume and the four would at some point bond. The whole time Nate was sitting and adding his thoughts to the conversation. He mostly just watched and he made eye contact with Juan. They both knew what Juan was doing, and Juan thought that he may have underestimated the X-preacher Nate, and that would not happen again.

The meeting and dinner went better than Juan had anticipated and his next undertaking was to get the mission started and organize everyone on the Gilgamesh mission to work in the same direction and with the same purpose. Once the mission was in progress the whole process would change as circumstances change, and some of this would be done on the fly. Most would be by design, and that's where Juan comes in and with his constant contact with Hanna Torres, they would get this mission on the road. Juan finally stepped in and said let's go over our mission objective. They all sat down and he took over and explained what he knew to date and where they would go from here, Juan explained that Hanna Torres was the Lead on this mission and that he was the field liaison. Juan went on to explain to the other players who were not on their side and that the intel he had on this other group was that they were funded and they had access to all the files. Also, the files that this other group has are not encrypted, but added that the files of this counter group have been fragmented. So they need to put what they have in sequence order so that they make sense. So the trip back to the States in its accelerated way was paramount and after Juan went through his presentation, the Gilgamesh team was excited and wanted to get started.

The plan was for them to enter the rental house as covertly as possible and at that time the group could not leave the premises until they had the secret files loaded into the Asgardians 777 computer. Juan had no idea how many files there were in the secret rooms. Once he saw them he would need to adjust the plan. They would have to cherry-pick the files that were relevant to what they were doing, and that would take some time. Especially with the mountain of files at the location. The idea was to work their way backward from the present, because that's where Juan thought the best and current data was.

The Gilgamesh team left the Mountain Top Villa and flew to the international airport. They had a charter plane ready for them, and the group made it through customs without a hitch. Their passports were as good as any out there and that wasn't an issue. On the plane, they were the only passengers and they could speak freely, because the crew were part of the Black Ops agency and they were trained not to listen. So each member had a job to do. It was decided that Yossele Schumacher be sent back to Israel so he could start his movement and search from there.Yossele would be given his directive before and after he arrived in his homeland. Because Yossele was an international traveler he could crisscross the globe using his many different Mossad ways or his business travel role. The whole time Yossele would have his shadows lurking in the background watching, protecting his flank.

Juan and company landed at the DuPage airport in Illinois with their lear jet, after they touched down and refueled in Miami FL. and went through customs. At the DuPage airport, the lear jet taxied to a hanger that was rented and used from time to time by this agency. The bird was driven into the hanger and the sliding door was closed behind it, to conceal the passengers. Sitting inside the very large hanger was a long black limo that would accommodate eight to ten passengers even though this group had just four. The security team that was always nearby would follow the limo from a distance in an obscure-looking Ford Expedition, that had four doors and dark windows. It would house 4 agents plus a driver for the protection of Juans Limo. Although they didn't expect any trouble they were always prepared and on alert, and ready to go to battle in a second.

The trip to the hotel went without a problem and the security squad set up residency in the adjoining room at the hotel, they would have their people loitering in the lobby and parked in the lot. Juan and Hanna knew how important this mission was, at least in their minds, and they left nothing to chance. The Gilgamesh team had no idea that they were protected in this manner, and that was by design. The group didn't need the stress, that was Juan's job.

After the group landed and settled into their hotel rooms they had a meeting set up, they met with Hanna Torres at her obscure-looking office and she went over her Itinerary, which wasn't much different than what Juan had laid out, and that was good. Hanna marked her spot drew a line in the sand and made it clear that She was the lead of this mission and she would make all decisions. With the exception of on the go, or changes that needed to be made. That would happen from time to time and they all knew it.

Hanna Torres, during the briefing, informed the group where she was on her research, what she and her superiors thought was going on, and why this group was made. She went on to do a show and tell and gave them all an individual folder, with the breakdown of the intel she has and where the Black Ops agency feels this thing is heading. She told them that there were thousands of secret labs working on stem cell research, virology, DNA, and blood type research all with the same file number or a fragment of it called BOJ-25:33, What Hanna found so far was the testing wasn't for anything she has heard off.She had just recently received intel that a select number of these labs with a secret part was also working on, or at least researching human cloning and that was not something that Hanna liked. When she revealed this latest data to the mission group, they were just as concerned, and the obvious questions are, what are we getting into, and where do you Hanna, think this is going? Hanna said she was not sure and wouldn't speak about something that she doesn't have facts. So they asked her what her gut feelings were and she said off the cuff, this whole secret research and development of a new virus or drug to cure viruses was dangerous. She thought that these labs were experimenting with what is called the GAIN OF FUNCTION concept and that's where an overactive virologist who has the funding of a large corporation and the secrecy, can take viruses from an animal that normally can't move or be transmitted from animal to human. These researchers find a way to mutate them and coax these sometimes deadly viruses to jump from animal to humankind. After these new viruses mutate they in many cases become so deadly and can be transmitted air-bound or by touch. After these researchers mutate these new and improved viruses that have just transversed the Gain of Function barrier, and the crossing of the species barrier from animal to human these same scientists try to find a cure to what they just created. Their thoughts are that at some time in the future these same viruses will mutate on their own and that we as humans need to be prepared.

Hanna went on to explain that at some point some governments, have stockpiles of thousands of deadly viruses that can be used for germ warfare. Hanna stated that with the intel she has, she can't be certain that this is what these labs are working on but, if not that, she feels they are working on something that, in her opinion should be left alone.

This team was on the threshold of fact-finding to follow the evidence wherever it took them, and the fact that they have the Mier Alter files may speed up the process.

Chapter 29

The File Room

The next day Juan sat down with his field group and Hanna Torres. They went over the day's agenda, which was the trip and more or less living at the Meir rental house until they could copy the hidden files.Hanna explained that there may be another group out there that has an interest in what she and the Gilgamesh team were doing. She went on to explain that this other entity wanted the same files that they were looking for and that she believed that this other group had more of the files than she had, and that this was a race against time. Hanna went on to explain that the Noah group was not some fly-by-night group and that they can be very dangerous, so their secrecy in living at the house needs to be just that. They as a group couldn't walk outside the home in the yard, because the house has been watched on and off from time to time. The rental needs to look just like it always does —empty— and the team understood, however, Bjoern was actually a civilian of sorts and had never gone through this kind of clandestine activity. He was at first excited, then giddy and the last emotion was fear. These were normal stages and Juan was watching for the signs and knew how to deal with them as Bjoern went through them one by one.Juan would enlist both Vonni and Nate to help Bjoern get through the last phase of this roller coaster emotional ride that all new members go through. Juan was sure that Bjoern would get over it with the support he had.

Bjoern led the others down into the lower level of the house and showed them the layout. No one could see the hidden rooms, and Bjoern at that point took out his key ring and started to slowly open the first hidden sliding wall to reveal the massive amount of files. Each column of files was dated by year and then by month, the team was in awe and this was just the first room. The group asked just how many of these were there, and Bjoern said he had located 11 and that some did not have as many files as this one. Some are very old, but Bjoern stated that the older files may or may not help them in this research. He thought that they should start at the last entry and work backward and they all agreed. So the last file that was dated just before the death of Meir Alter was pulled and examined and to the group's dismay it was in the same written code on the flash drive that Bjoern had shown them in South America. They would open several other files and each one was in a similar code and they all groaned that this undertaking was going to be enormous. Just copying the files to the Asgardians 777 computer would take time, even with the state-of-the-art scanner. Juan assured his team that although this is a mountain of data they are actually looking for a small amount of information, and that starting at the last entry was the best chance of finding the documents they wanted.

At the bottom of each page of every file was a peculiar phase that showed just like this α Ω +,- 1111+(0,1,1,2,3,5,8,13,21,34,55,89,144,233)#+-%~* and made no sense to anyone, however this same phasing was at the bottom of each page or the beginning of the file and, this marking drew interest from everyone in the group but Bjoern. Mostly because he wasn't in spy mode just yet, and the others were in tune with almost everything that was going on. They tried not to let even the smallest clue pass without making a mental note of what they saw and sometimes they would bring the clue to the other's attention so they could all discuss it. This phase was intriguing and as a group, they felt it was important.

The Asgardians 777 was put to work and the phase ᾳ Ὠ +,- 1111+(0,1,1,2,3,5,8,13,21,34,55,89,144,233)#+-%~* was scanned into the system for it to work on. The files that were the most current were entered one by one and the machine was doing its thing working on each file that was loaded in. The 777 can work on multiple files at the same time without suffering a slowdown or errors in any way. The group had invested the whole day scanning the files in just this one room, however, they couldn't load them all and would have to wait for the 777 to accept additional data. It was working on about four large encrypted files at this time. The amount of CPU working on the existing files was taxing, and for the best quickest results, it was better to limit the amount of encryption data that the 777 was working on. The timeline was going to be a lot longer than anticipated, unless they caught a break, during this time Hanna Torres was still working on her end putting together the flash drives she receives daily to help with her Gilgamesh team's work and research. At some point, the files that Hanna has and her mission team have will have to be laid side by side to put this puzzle together. The files that Juan's team has entered so far may take several hours for the 777 to decode, and hopefully, the file's accuracy will be higher than the 72 percent they have on the first flash drive from Bjoern.Juan also knew that in time as new encoded files were worked on by the 777 the software would revert back to the original flash drive and recompute its contents. This computer would block learn and adapt as it went and get smarter, and as time went on and the 777 got better the software would do the files over and over in its effort to achieve a 100 percent accuracy. The ᾳ Ὠ +,- 1111+(0,1,1,2,3,5,8,13,21,34,55,89,144,233

)#+-%~* phrase listed on each file was being worked on by the 777s software and was trying to make a connection between the phrase and the files. Hanna's thoughts were that this particular set of numbers and notes were important and maybe a key of sorts to unlocking the code that was so difficult to unlock.

The Gilgamesh team was all sitting at a large table and looking through the many files that were already scanned. They noticed that the shorthand typewriting was different from one file to the next and sometimes different from page to page. Since Vonni was the only one who had experience in shorthand scribe she looked at the files and was at first confused because she couldn't read any of the wording or notes. Vonni kept reading or trying to, and she made an interesting discovery. That the shorthand writing that was not readable as shorthand she found that from one page to the next the writing seemed to change to a different language. Then she thought that the writing not only changed from one language to another but also to the different styles of shorthand, like Teeline, Pitman, and the Gregg methods. She knew that if the 777 could make heads or tails of this all while being coded, then the computer was truly a piece of equipment that shouldn't be in bad actors' hands. Vonni was thinking to herself how could any man come up with this coding system and then without a computer read it, what kind of mind would that take? She was in awe of Meir Alter's ability, and she was sure that this was just scratching the surface of this man's intellect.

The Asgardians 777 would take several more hours of work to decode what it has and make a brief for Hanna and the Gilgamesh team. During this time Hanna was putting her inside team to work on what they had and Hanna would have an assignment for Yossele once he had arrived back in

Israel. That assignment would be to look at and do his Mossad black Ops on several labs in the Middle East that Hanna doesn't have a mole or access to. Yossele Schumacher received the assignment, and he and his team could move anywhere in the world at a moment's notice. He looked at the labs in question and thought that he may have some people close to these labs, if not inside at least close to some of the technicians that worked at them. So Yossele started his mission and he put his agents in place at the first lab that Hanna Torres wanted to be looked at. He traveled to the country of Niger where he would try to access the lab's computer for what Hanna wanted. This country like so many in the region are poor and have a series of coups and political instability, and bribing personnel at a lab could be done with enough money. Access to the computers could be given as Yossele was a master at underhanded dealing and bribery. It was commonplace for Black Ops, and Mossad to gain information, and Nigers labs wouldn't be any different. These labs would be the first on his list of many to get the intel that Hanna needed, and she hoped that what Yossele could attain would be purer than what she had received from her moles in the other labs.

Chapter 30

BOJ-25:33 File And The Need For Speed

Damek Hava caught wind of the Gilgamesh mission, and he didn't like that at all. What he didn't know was the existence of the very special computer and software called Asgardians 777.Damek was briefed on some of the players in the mission. He will keep tabs on this new group that's showing interest in his business. Damek let his team, the Knights of Noah know of the new development and the additional players in his quest for the elusive BOJ-25:33 file. Damek would, in his way encourage the Noah group to pick up the pace on their investigation and research, and add additional agents and that cost was not an issue. Damek also would enlist the Noah group's own version of the Valhalla hit squad that was so infamous and efficient. The Noah group had their version that was left in a dormant state, and the hit men and women could be activated at any given time. At present, this team was on alert, that just meant that they could be called up at a moment's notice. The Noah group administrator, or leader put his best people on the alert status, and gave them a mini brief as to what they would be sent out to do and where. With the brief, the Noah's secret hit Squad called Diablo Djinn, are on call and is seldom used but they are ruthless and have never failed in their assignments.

The Damek point man, Fredrich Becker was getting more and more of the puzzle. With the assistance of his research partner, Frieda Von Helm, the process was picking up speed, and the constant updates that he sent to Damek were encouraging. Fredrich tried to emphasize the sheer struggle of this crusade, but Damek didn't want to hear that kind of talk.

Fredrich and Frieda had so far put together quite a starter file that looked promising and seemed to be on track. With everything they have so far from the labs and Damek, they could extrapolate where the BOJ-25:33 file and cure were going so that they could steer the research in that direction. Unfortunately for the Gilgamesh group, they didn't have as much raw data. All they had was what Hanna Torres had and a boatload of encrypted files that none of the groups knew would shed any light on what their mission was. But they had the 777 that was working and they had the original files and the time to decipher was anyone's guess.

Yossele was in Niger working on the lab technicians and trying to get the data that was in the mainframe computers. Yossele had made decent contact, with one person who was high up in the lab's administration, and for the right amount of American Dollars, the man would copy everything that was requested of him and deliver it. What Yossele wasn't aware of was the data was in medical jargon and the test results were as well. For him, it wasn't a smoking gun, but Yossle would forward the very large file to Hanna Torres for her to work on. This betrayal of the lab's security didn't go unnoticed by the Noah group and who the administrator gave the hard drive to. They informed their employer Damek and he was enraged because they should have stopped the transfer of the data. He gave the order that they are permitted to do whatever it took to stop that kind of breach again wherever the Noah agents find it, and the Noah group is authorized to use whatever method they see fit to keep the lab files secret. That meant the use of the Diablo Djinn squads. The Knights of

Noah activated the secret hit men and they would get assembled and wait for instructions for the assignment.

Hanna Torres received the large hard drive and started to integrate the data into her system. As she always did, she took the files and assembled them in her way and on the jumble screen. She would move the files around back and forth almost like a game show. Hanna worked deep into the night and the next day when she was satisfied with what she had and in the correct order, that's when Hanna would sit back and absorb the whole screen and its contents and study what she had. Again she has put the pattern in focus, and what she has so far was interesting and added it to the big picture. But still, she didn't know where this whole caper was going to end up. She had an idea but she didn't work on ideas, Hanna worked on facts, and she wanted, she needed the files at the rental house decoded. She was sure that somewhere in that basement full of files was the answer. Hanna was getting anxious, and that was common for her. The energy she received from that emotion propelled her forward and seldom was there anyone who could keep up with her pace when she was on a fact-finding quest. Especially when she is on a scent or what some would say she would sense blood in the water. Hanna was indeed a shark of sharks in her field. What she saw in the files so far was that this particular lab was working on a virus that was tested over and over in so many different ways that she was astounded that so much time and resources were invested in the testing. This made her even more curious.

Hanna had what she needed from this lab in Niger and she wanted information from several others in that country. She would send Yossele his next assignment and which labs she needed data from.

Hanna discovered that this first lab was doing the testing of the HERVs or Human endogenous retroviruses, these viruses are ancient viral infections that humanity suffered from, and this infection became part of the DNA. They are called retroviruses and are dormant or are not a problem because they are part of the human genomes. However, labs and researchers have discovered that the HERV Genes are active in diseased tissue such as tumors as well as during human embryonic development, but how active is still unknown. Again these retroviruses are passed down through generations and Hanna was stunned and wondered why a lab would be working on an ancient, retrovirus that doesn't harm the human race. This kind of testing is unheard of and it piqued her interest to the point that Hanna will watch for this activity in the new data she receives. This revelation or breakthrough in her search for the answers to the end game has her stumped, Hanna still was at a loss where this was going, but she knew she was onto something big.

The Asgardians 777 software has completed two of the four files and will not complete a brief, pending the completion of all of them. Mostly because as the 777 finished each file it got smarter, and as it did the software would go over the previous files to update and adjust for accuracy, at present the 777 was now up to 79 percent accurate. Up 7 percent and that was unacceptable in any venue but it was a start and Juan knew that the 777 would get better in time. He just hoped that they had the time.Juan had this feeling that he sometimes got when a mission went sideways and the outcome wasn't what he hoped for.Juan kept this feeling of dread to himself as usual but at the same time would quicken the pace if, at all possible. His long private conversations with Hanna about what was proceeding on her end didn't help his demeanor. Juan and Hanna were on the same page when it came to the urgency of this mission, and

Juan in the field working with for the most part untested civilians made his job that much more difficult.

Chapter 31

Asgardians 777, Secrets

The Laptop with the Asgardians 777 software the super chip and drives, which have a storage capacity beyond most mainframe military computers have, has secret decoding software. This software has been tested and retested and has been extremely effective at breaking every coded document that has been entered, this machine is so advanced and secret that only a select few in the U.S. government even know of its existence. The updates and improvements are in constant flux and movement. The 777 worked its magic on the 4 large files that were loaded into it. As it was in a quandary with the encryption and at best the accuracy was sitting right at the 80 percentile. For this software and its ability, this has never happened, and Juan was astounded. But he would look at what the computer had at this point and convey the accuracy and brief to Hanna Torres.

The inaccurate files show at this time that Meir Alter was indeed working on a cure and that he had perfected it and had made the completed procedure on how to go about administering this new cure for a disease that as it turns out, is now genetic, and at one time was not part of the gnomic coding of the afflicted group that has the disease. The particular disease was caused by the mutation of a gene in this group's gene pool, and was specific to this one group only. What some would call a very unique and singular gene mutation. What the brief showed was that the gene mutation may have been caused by an ancient virus that has gone dormant, but has deposited some of its DNA into the subjects base genes. What Juan didn't understand was why this mutation in a genetic pool was centered around or to this select group only and hadn't affected anyone else. From what Juan could see in the brief, the amount of people who were affected was over a hundred thousand and the exact number was unknown because the 777 could not come up with that number just yet. However, Meir Alter states he has come up with a cure, and from what the limited accuracy of the encrypted files shows was that the cure was somewhere in the other files, and that may take time to find. The next issue was the accuracy, and Juan was hopeful that as time and files were entered this would improve. The 777 didn't give a name for the cure or its file name so the process of scanning and letting the 777 decode and work was going to require more time than they expected. , So at this point since Yossele was investigating labs in Niger and doing well, Juan would confer with Hanna Torres and what his group should be doing during the file decoding.

Hanna and Juan decided that the Gilgamesh team should be in the field and that they could serve the mission better. Hanna decided that from the data that she has from numerous labs, and the way things are coming together she wanted something looked at that was a bit off the beaten path, and seemed at this point not related to this mission.Hanna wanted the Gilgamesh team to do research and then get hands-on with missing persons across the world. In most cases, this would be an impossible undertaking, because of the sheer number of missing people. But Hanna had a plan as usual, she had criteria she wanted to follow, and the first part for researching missing persons was age, then gender, and race, country, and last was blood type. Hanna had the exact criteria she wanted to be followed, and although she didn't have scientific bases for her bracketing, as usual, because of Hanna's unique thought process she was given carte blanche. The Gilgamesh team was all too eager to get involved in the new mission. Nate stated that he has some experience in this area because he has been working on missing people and children in South America, and has a sort of network going down there with Law enforcement and other groups, and this may help with some of the searches.

The Gilgamesh team went to work on sorting and organizing the mountain of missing people in the world and narrowed the search pattern down to what Hanna's category was. This would take time but they were busy and would get the crew working as a team, and that was important.

Hanna would take the data that her team assembled on missing persons and refine that group again in private. Hanna didn't want to let anyone know what her thoughts were until she had the facts.As Hanna received the reports with everything listed she would refine the list by blood type, and then age and blood type, then age blood type and gender, and last but not least by age, blood type, gender, and race. Hanna wanted to see if there was an interrelationship between the select groups. When she had them all broken down Hanna would see which ones crossed the lines and were in more than a single group. She would focus on anyone that crossed and then she looked at any that crossed multiple lines. Hanna had an idea of what she was looking for and hoped she was wrong. As more and more missing people were entered and categorized her suspicions became clearer and she didn't like what she was seeing. Hanna would put this new file data on the Jumbo screen and as she dropped it on the screen she would have to readjust some of the files. As the domino effect of one file changes they all need realignment and she would move them to the order that made sense to her. The puzzle was coming together. Hanna knew she would require a lot more data before she had the whole picture but she liked where the team was going and the results that were coming in. Hanna could see that the speed was increasing and she was waiting for the intel from Yossele and anything that the 777 could kick out from the 4 new folders that were scanned in. What Hanna wasn't aware of was that the Asgardians 777 software was working on the four large folders/files and the system was deciphering and decoding three of the 4 files in the expected time frame, however, one of these files was giving the Asgardians 777 a tough time and it was investing more of its memory, and processing ability to this very exceptional file. The other three were all but complete at the 80 percent accuracy mark. The 777 would kick out the brief on what it has with a warning per se, that one of the files may be unbreakable, and that the 777 will continue to slave over the file and try to break its file. The only two coherent writing that the 777 has on this mysterious and seemingly unbreakable file is its name designation and which is Bereshit 1—,(in Hebrew, means in the beginning) and the phrase (ᶏ Ω+,- 1111+(0,1,1,2,3,5,8,13,21,34,55,89,144,233)#+-%~*). That's virtually all the 777 has on this massive file that is as large as a terabyte of data. As more and more processing ability is available because the other three files are complete the 777 will devote the entire resources of its systems to crack and decipher what the Bereshit 1, and phrase/coding file has hidden in it. The 777 has been looking at the special phrase listed on so many pages and the 777 was starting to see something in the phrase/code the 777 looked at this as a code but couldn't break it, and that was because the ᶏ Ω+,- 1111+(0,1,1,2,3,5,8,13,21,34,55,89,144,233)#+-%~* is in code but is the actual key to all the written data that are in code. The 777 was starting to see this for what it was and reevaluate this key and how to use it. Before the 777 produced a brief on this file, a micro brief was printed with what the 777 was on to and that it was now working on the key decoding. The last file received the attention it deserved from Juan and he sent the new data to his counterpart Hanna Torres. The two sat together in a conference room and they both felt that this file was the Holy Grail of files or at least a good beginning. They would allocate another 24 hours of processing time for the 777 to work exclusively on this file.This was a waiting game and it was also full of actions. Several different events were going on at the same time across the world, and Hanna knew that her Gilgamesh team would need to be in the field soon. With the 777 working for the next 24 hours on this one file, Hanna would put her team to work on a new missing person angle and her newest approach to the missing person's selection or elimination from her study group was that she wants the search narrowed down now to an age group. Race and gender weren't an issue, but Hanna would require the perimeters to tighten and only include a certain set of blood types.Hanna's thought process was that she could reduce or expand that criterion later if needed. Hanna wanted the blood types of ab negative, and ab positive and the most important blood type she was interested in was rh-null, commonly called the Golden Blood. This particular blood is the rarest in the world as fewer than 500 people in the world have this blood type. At least that's what the scientists believe. The actual number of people with this rh-null may be significantly higher, and Hanna has one of her hunches that the secret labs are working on a specific specimen or lab rats as some of the human test subjects are referred to.

Chapter 32

Mission Contact Persons

Yossele had made his contact with another lab in Niger and through his whining and dining received a nugget of information from Administrator Abioye Fayola. He believed that there was another hidden secret lab that was completely off the books and this lab was located somewhere in the dense jungles of Africa. The exact location was not known. Yossele pressed this administrator for additional information and he said he would inquire about this secret lab, but that it was very dangerous.Yossele knew that meant additional funds or American dollars. He had no problem with that because he had a good budget for this sort of thing. So Yossele assured his new contact that if the information was good and useful then the man would receive a substantial reward. Since there is honor among thieves, the two had a deal. The insider would do his research for the exact location and any additional information he could uncover.

Abioye Fayola, quietly did his research using his mainframe company computer to locate the hidden secret lab that he had heard of. After much research, he found a file that was in the archive, or it was put there as a way to bury it. He pulled the file and its sub-files and copied them to a thumb drive.He hid the drive in his Yoruba Cap, commonly known as a Fila (hat) or headdress. The way the hat is worn will indicate if the man is married or single. Abioye was able to smuggle the thumb drive out without a problem. He hid the drive at his townhouse and he put it in a very hidden area that was in plain sight and still hidden.Abioye reviewed the data that was downloaded, and he was curious about what he was reading. He was amazed to find that this secret lab housed several hundreds of patients. These people were of a certain age group. Abioye Fayola, besides being curious became greedy and would say that the data and file that he has was worth more than originally bargained for. Abioye would have to reopen renegotiations.

Abioye made contact with Yossele and they sat down to dinner at a secluded Niger restaurant.That's when Abioye informed Yossele that he had what the Mossad agent wanted and that he had it on a flash drive at his house. However, Abioye stated he reviewed all the data and could see that this information was more than the two of them thought it was. Because of the importance of this new intel, Abioye believed that the flash drive was worth twice the last agreed amount.Yossele stated that if what's on the drive is as good as Abioye says it is he will agree to payment. Before they broke for the day and agreed to meet the next day Abioye told Yossele that he hid the drive in plain sight at his townhouse, and unless you were a religious man you would never find it.

Damek Hava received information that Abioye was looking at the file and that he may have copied it, and Damek sent his henchmen out to retrieve the drive and eliminate Abioye Fayola. He was killed in their usual way, an icepick to the back of the brain, quick and almost no noise and he was put sitting in a reclining chair so he looked like he was asleep. Very little seepage came from the wound. The Noah group liked that, and the fact that the search area was clean and not a bloody mess.Damek wouldn't stand for that kind of data leak and he sent the Knights of Noah to take out the garbage.From the intel that Damek has, Abioye has not been able to pass the drive on to anyone and that was good. The hitmen did their jobs and made a thorough search of Abioye's home but couldn't find the flash drive, and had to give up the search when the sun started to come up. The exterminators didn't want to be discovered.

Yossele called Abioye Fayola the next day to exchange the second part of the bribe, and exchange the flash drive but there was no answer. This didn't sit well with Yossele because he knew that Abioye Fayola was waiting for his call and the cell went directly to voicemail. Yossele made his way cautiously to where Abioye lived and he used a cab to drive past the residence. That's when he saw the ambulance and police cars sitting out front and at that point, Yossele knew that the administrator's life was gone. Yossele's next thoughts were of the thumb drive and the fact that it was hidden in what Abioye said was in plain sight. He hoped that this piece of information wasn't found by the Noah group that Yossele was sure was behind the assassination. He would have to bide his time and lean on some police as to how the investigation was going. Yossele would have his people stake out Abioye Fayola's house from a distance and keep track of everyone that came and went during business hours and especially at night. But this didn't pan out, as the Knight of Noah had left the area because they believed that the thumb drive wasn't on the premises.Yossele's thoughts were that the Noah group would have their team watch the house day and night just as Yossele had, so for Yossele to do his own search would prove difficult, but not impossible. Again Yossele was a master at this sort of thing and his Mossad team located the Noah watch team and kept tabs on them as well. Yossele entered the home of the deceased Abioye Fayola after a couple of nights of no action when the Noah team got sloppy in their surveillance.

Yossele looked around the home and saw that it was trashed and everything was turned upside down and was thoroughly searched by the Noah team, and then by the police. Yossele could see the telltale signs that the police were looking for fingerprints and the usual type of mess the authorities leave, Yossele started his search. He kept in mind the last words that Abioye Fayola said to him about the flash drive. That he hid it in plain sight and the keywords were If you are not religious you may never find it. That stuck in Yossele's thoughts, so he didn't look in the same places that the Noah group did. He just stood there and looked around and gave it a lot of thought and as he was looking around the family room he noticed a religious artifact on the wall. It was a wooden crucifix that just hung there askew and was very thin and unobtrusive at best. The cross caught Yossele's eye, because in Africa and Yoruba tradition, half Muslim and about half Christian, and Yossele thought that Abioye was a Muslim, so a wooden cross didn't fit in. As he carefully removed the cross from the wall he made sure that it wasn't booby-trapped. That's good Mossad training. Yossele examined the artifact and it looked normal, but at a certain angle, he could see a small line or crack in the lower portion of the cross. He tried to wiggle it or pry on it and as he did a piece of the wooden cross fell free and revealed a hidden compartment, almost like what you might see when you have two triple aaa batteries under a plastic sliding panel.Yossele examined the removed portion of wood and nothing was there he looked deeper into the base of the crucifix and could see another compartment deeper up the shaft of the cross, Yossele removed his stiletto knife from his pocket and pushed the button and the blade jumped out and gleamed in the dark light of the room. The only light that Yossele had was the Mossad-style headlight on his forehead that he could control with either a white, yellow, or red light, he switched it to spotlight in the white color and picked at the compartment that he could just make out. A hidden trap door popped open and fell out and that's when Yossele could clearly see the flash drive. Even with his vast years of experience, and being a Mossad agent his heart raced. This was not the norm for him but he was excited and he tapped the wooden cross on his palm and the drive fell into his hand.He just looked at it and thought what could be on this piece of equipment that would warrant a death sentence? Because of that fact and thought Yossele knew why his heart was racing. He was aware of the danger he was now in. His survival mode kicked in and he went into full stealth mode. He put his headlight to dim red, and he now was as quiet as a mouse and he was on full alert. Yossele's next move was to get out of this house unnoticed and alive. Yossele made his way to the back door and discreetly looked out and with his trained eyes he watched for several minutes for any signs of movement or other dangers. After about thirty minutes he signaled his watch team that he was coming out and that they should be on high alert for any bad actors that may be watching. After Yossele got the green light he made his way out of the back door and slowly made his way to the support group he had in the background.

Yossele looked at the thumb drive he retrieved and he just turned the device over and over in his fingers. Again he thought, what could be so important on this that would warrant killing an administrator of a lab? Yossele would share the contents of the drive with the Gilgamesh team and he would at the same time send a copy home to the Mossad. After that, he would take the time and examine the data that was on the drive. Yossele needed to know the full contents of the drive and not the briefed version that the 777 or Hanna Torres would give out. If nothing else, Yossele was meticulous in everything he did as a Mossad, and that has kept him alive so far.

Yossele opened and read the contents of the flash drive as he sat at his desk in his hotel room. He knew this would take some time to digest and he would set aside the time he required. As he read file after file, Yossele would get more and more disturbed by the data he was reading. His Mossad mind started to assemble a scenario that he didn't like, and he hoped he was wrong and way off base. Yossele was seldom wrong, but he hoped that this time he was.

Chapter 33

BOJ-25:33 File Assembly

As Dameks scientist, Fredrich Becker worked on the cure and what files he has to date, he was getting a better understanding and handle on what he was working on. Fredrich at some point spoke to Damek via encrypted email and asked for full disclosure from his employer. He stated that he is loyal and that Damek knew what Fredrich's history and past was. Fredrich received a response from Damek that all would become clear, and that Fredrich would be told everything. Damek knew that at some point, his new scientist would need to know everything and be brought in. Even though that bothers Damek he was sure that he could take care of anything that might become embarrassing or detrimental to the cause or to his family. Damek also knew the family history of Fredrich Becker and the fact that his grandfather was Reinhard Heydrich in the Nazi German military. That fact gave Damek the feeling that this grandson was just as ruthless.

Fredrich Becker received the additional secret data from Damek in small portions and just enough to keep him in the loop but not the whole story. Trust has to be earned.

The amount of new data that Fredrich had received from all sources would make his job easier because he now had a better picture of the finished product. However, he was still in the dark in so many other areas. That was the way Damek wanted it.

Fredrich and his assistant or cohort, Frieda Von Helm have been getting the data sorted and put in order. All the files with the designation BOJ-25:33 were starting to take shape. They were starting to see what the cure should look like, but were still missing some of the key numbers and data to make it work. The two could now see where Meir Alter was heading and the end results. Both of them were amazed at the sheer intellect of this man. Damek was informed that they thought that they were within reach of the final product, or the complete procedure and technique for making the BOJ-25:33 cure. But they would need additional time and some more documents. They thought that these documents were on the way.

The BOJ-25:33 cure from the twosome's perspective was the single most profound medical breakthrough they have seen in history. With Frieda Von Helm's history of working on human cloning, she was very interested in the research that she was reading. With the DNA testing and splicing that has been accomplished, she thought that this was years ahead of modern cloning. Frieda was absorbing everything she read and could follow the different testing as it went from one failure to the next, and then to some success, and then to the final successful product.

Frieda read how DNA was manipulated, spliced, and in a controlled mutated form.Frieda also read that these tests were mostly done on human subjects. At first glance, this caught her off guard, and after a short time, she said to herself, that it was the fastest, best way to achieve the results needed for a cure. She also thought that sometimes there have to be sacrifices. If that meant a few thousand people would have to give their lives for the world she had no problem doing testing on live humans. Her mentality was that we send people to war to give up their lives for the many, this is no different.

The BOJ-25:33 cure was thought to be within their grasp and the two researchers believed they would have the final product within 10-14 days. This made Damek Hava breathe easier or settle down a bit, but Damek was still very concerned about this Gilgamesh team out there. He would put that to rest with his goon squad, the Knights of Noah, and order the elimination of said group. They needed to recover all data they had if possible.

The Gilgamesh team was working in unison on the mission, and as the laptop with the software 777 was still working on the fourth file that was proving to be a challenge to this one-of-a-kind computer, the 777 was making progress.Juan was wondering why the 777 was having such difficulty on the last file they loaded and he typed in a request for a possible resolution to the issue. He wanted a brief as to the reason, the 777 is having difficulty. The Asgardians 777 printed a detailed docket as to why the time frame is taking longer than expected. The reason was that the file in question was quite large, encrypted, and in several different languages. But the 777 showed that this was not the roadblock. The docket spelled out exactly what the software was facing.When the original file was opened it had 7 sub files. Each of these files was in what is called a lockbox, and in a lockbox, the data is encrypted and scattered throughout the flash drive. So the 777 would decode the first lockbox security password and the file would open. Inside the lock box was another set of three lockboxes all with their own set of passwords. As the 777 deciphered another box, the newly opened lockbox would have three more lock boxes and that would go on for 11 sequences. That's just the first file in a set of 7 subfiles and the last opened files would have information that pertained to the BOJ-

25:33 File and how the tests were done. However, the file would be just short of a complete formula making the opening of all 7 subfiles and all lockboxes important. It's like a sea of lockboxes that need to be worked on one at a time. Each one has its own password, and that takes time to decode. The Asgardians 777 at this point has opened about half of the lockboxes in all 7 subfiles and the information was starting to accumulate. At this point, it was more or less just data, and no one could make sense of what half of the information meant. Juan could see they were on the right track and he made contact with Hanna Torres. He informed her of the hold-up and delay. Hanna wished she had what the 777 had so far but Juan said that was virtually impossible at this time. Juan had high hopes that the 777 would complete the work within the next several days. In the meantime, Hanna Torres received the data from the flash drive that Yossele had retrieved and was processing that as well. She would include it in her daily briefing to her Gilgamesh team and detail what the next plans would be. At this time, that may be determined by what she reads from the new data and Hanna will confer with Juan as well. Hanna wanted the data that was hidden on that fourth file, which was so adeptly hidden from anyone's view. Hanna knew more and more of the pieces of the puzzle were coming together and had high hopes for the Yossele data flash drive. Hanna was fully aware of the assassination of the lab administrator and this was a wake-up call that her team was getting close. She would need to step up security for her team in her own covert way.Hanna would inform Yossele what she was doing. If he didn't feel comfortable with her security then he should let her know that he was providing his own. It wouldn't do well if her people were injured by friendly fire and vice-versa. For Yossele's agents, that's just good business.

Hanna opened the data stream she received from Yossele and read it and sat back in her very cushy desk chair. What she read was not what she expected. The intel showed that there were other so-called secret labs out there, and these respective labs were anything but. They were essentially compounds, or what some would call a Goulash. These compounds housed people that were being used as human guinea pigs or test subjects. The amount of victims that were housed in these labs was restricted to a control number that was kept at this amount. Some for cross-contamination and some for control, the actual number of test subjects was always kept at the number 333. That didn't include the researchers and other support people. What the data showed was that the age group of the test subjects was always below the 30-year-old mark and no younger than 12. These individuals were told that they all had a terrible plague and that if they were to leave the compound and stop receiving the medication they would certainly die. The 333 people were convinced that the tale was true and they all worked in the compound to make it better. They did tasks like laundry, cleaning, cooking, schooling, and other jobs so they would stay busy. This was part of a plan to keep the people occupied so they didn't question the situation they were in, what the tests were, or when they could leave. This flash drive that Yossele retrieved also had locations of other labs or compounds of the same kind and what these other labs were working on.

Hanna sat back in her chair as she was formulating her team's next assignment. She was worried because this was bigger than she could envision.

The testing that was being performed at the compounds was all different and in a way the same. The labs were infecting their test group with its' own assigned virus and then curing them. This testing would allow the virus to mutate. The labs were looking at that mutation. The virus DNA that was left behind attached to humans. They would watch the transformation of the new or altered DNA and examine the new sequence. The secret labs had developed a way of curing, or in essence, putting a virus in a dormant/sleep mode inactive, or what is called Latent infection. What these labs were doing secretly was triggering their viruses to become active at a given time or at their discretion. The way they finally discovered the procedure for the trigger mechanism was to use another virus to induce the latent virus to undergo a reactivation phase where it begins to replicate and infect cells causing a repeat infection. The labs were looking for a common virus that they could mutate into the trigger virus and each of the many labs were working on the same thing but using different deadly viruses and different virus triggers. These labs have to date several prototypes of the experimental virus. The labs have been switching over from their assigned virus research to the prototype virus and the other labs tested a different prototype. They tested the new mutated virus that they had decided to mutate from an animal virus and caused this virus to the Gain of Function sequence, and the human barrier was removed.

The labs all started to work on this one method of turning on the dormant virus. They discovered that the human body has ancient viruses' DNA strands left in them from thousands of years ago. Some of the DNA that is still there can be made to replicate, and the ancient virus would be active. These labs looked hard and long at the Spanish Flu that killed 50 million and many other deadly viruses such as the Bubonic plague and so many others. What they did was engineer a completely new virus that would be inactive in the human body and be more or less benign. However, when this new virus was introduced into the body it was harmless. When the trigger virus was introduced an Antigenic Shift occurred. The process of two or more viruses combining to form a new subtype that would have the properties of the joined viruses. The two would become not only deadly, but now extremely virulent. The virus of choice would be airborne in transmission. They found that the second virus would also need to be transmitted in the same manner. This transmission design on the Antigen Shift was a prerequisite, or requirement from the owner of the Labs. Damek Hava and his number one scientist Meir Alter. That was the direction the labs received and that's how they all tested and experimented on the delivery system. This new virus would cause a human to first become sleepy, and fall into a deep sleep almost coma state. Then the virus would attack the respiratory system and cause the lungs to hemorrhage. Because the victim is unconscious they couldn't help with their recovery. The Labs found that this very precise virus was effective, or deadly to 90 percent of the world's population, and the survivors were of a special blood type, or gene sequence or genotypes. This made Damek happy because he liked the percentages and this would fit into his final plan.

Chapter 34

The Missing Persons Research

Nate Williams, the ex-priest and social worker who is part of the Gilgamesh team and Divine Activity mission is involved with many police agencies in South America. In the recent past, he had put together a program to track the lost or missing people across the continent. This proved to be difficult getting different countries and their law enforcement to cooperate. However, with Nate's unique way of convincing people what he was doing was good for each country as well as others, and after a lot of red tape, Nate was able to receive the data from almost all the countries in South America. And as was determined by Hanna Torres, he would reduce the mountain of data down to a certain criteria. That was by age and blood type. The list was narrowed down considerably. Nate would also eliminate any subjects that were recovered by death or came back home or were imprisoned. Again the list became shorter. Nate was able to access the world database of missing people. He put in the same parameters and the missing persons list was staggering. Nate was overwhelmed. He knew he would need to reduce the search pattern down to a manageable number. He again changed the search purviews with just a couple of blood types. He used the types that were the rarest, AB+,- A+, B-, and of course the most rare blood type of them all, Rh null known as the golden blood type. Once he did that the list was manageable. The reason that Nate was doing this research was that his team leader Juan and his superior Hanna believed that the lab compounds that housed the virus test subjects were in fact missing persons at one time, and more or less forgotten, or at least not on the radar anymore. This was Hanna's hunch and they went with it, with hopes they could get the identities of the living test subjects that are in the secret labs across the globe. This reduction or lessening of the type of people could help in determining the direction the testing was progressing. In time Hanna was sure she would figure out what they were testing for exactly. Hanna could sense that some or all of the virus testing had a determinate link to DNA. Hanna was looking at possible links to cloning or some part of that process. What Hanna did know was that every time a different virus was introduced into the body, DNA from the virus was left behind and that the human body's DNA was about 8 percent made up of retroviruses. Hanna thought there was some connection. She would have to confer with a specialist on this matter for a better picture, but she didn't like what her data told her at this point. She would require more, and she wanted that last dam file that the 777 was working on.

The missing person search was exhausting and Nate was working hard on it when he had an idea that maybe this was more than just random missing persons. Nate's thoughts were, could the missing people have something more in common? He saw the blood type correlation, and that didn't sit well. So Nate would look at the medical records of the shortened lists of missing people. When he did a large number would come back with the same blood type. All of them had recently gone to their doctor and had blood tests done recently. These blood tests were sent to labs that were either owned or had strong affiliations with the secret labs.When Nate found this information he dug deeper and tried to narrow done the time frame from blood tests to missing persons. The time frame was astounding. Nate discovered that anyone that matched the criteria that he put forward, would be a missing person within thirty days of the labs testing. Nate continued his research and looked for anyone who might be involved in the missing persons. He could see a pattern that he thought the individuals may have been abducted and weren't just missing. With this new information, he presented the data to Juan. Juan sent the file up to Hanna Torres. Even though she had some thoughts on the same track, Hanna now had the data she could put up on her Jumbo screen. At that time she would need to re-arrange the files to fit where she liked them. This was good work by Nate, and he was given better access to the dark web than would be given to any civilian. This access would open a lot more doors for Nate's research. Now he could look at financial records, rental cars, and even secret safe houses that the opposition or bad guys have. Nate would dive in, and his research would improve. He was sickened by what he was learning. The Dark Web would locate and determine that there was an underground group that would abduct a particular blood type or DNA structure. This would again confuse Nate. He determined that the abductors seemed to have two different factions. One that wanted just the certain blood types and age groups, and another that was more gene and DNA-driven. So Nate established that this Shanghai group had two or more businesses that they were working with, and the abductions were multi-faceted in a way that every one of the abductees would find a placement. These people were just a commodity for the abduction business they were in and they were very specific on who they took. It was never anyone with money or influence and they never asked for ransom. These people were more or less just cattle and used as such. The money that each abductee could generate was astronomical. The yearly amount is in excess of one hundred and fifty billion dollars, and reports are that the U.S. is one of the largest contributors to the trade. The syndicate had to be very selective. That was easy because they worked under the radar and no one looked for them or knew they existed. They called themselves Mongols, a name from the originals that did it in the 12th century. No abductee would go to waste. Every one of them generated revenue for the Mongo's.Damek Hava was a frequent client, because his lab Compounds needed additional recruitments as tests were completed. Some were fatal, and that happened more times than not.

The secret Damek labs have started to work on the new mutated virus that was called Jud-12:6,(Shibboleth) and they were making an incredible amount of the Vaccine for this mutated virus that was all but a mild form of flu. But the Vax could be administered airborne. However, it could also be administered through the usual way of the normal vax injection that almost everyone receives calling it the yearly flu shot. This new virus was the one that Damek was counting on to complete the progression of the cure. He knew the cure was just days away from being his. Damek was getting all his ducks in a roll and he calculated that the amount of the Vax needed to do what he wanted was going to be a lot. This unique Jud-12:6 Virophages type is a group of double-stranded DNA-based viruses that infect and kill other viruses.Damek Hava knew this would aid in the elimination of HERVS (human endogenous retroviruses) that make up around 8 percent of the human genome left behind as a result of infections that our human Primate ancestors suffered thousands of years ago, and became part of the genome due to how they replicate. One of these ancient viruses is what has caused the inherited disease his family has. This particular affliction had a very specific DNA and would only attack a certain sequence or type and no other. That is why some people inherit diseases. Damek's family has the only known affliction like this. His family's DNA is unique, and was not shared over the many years of their existence. That's the reason why he wants the cure. The Jud-12:6, mutated virus was a designer virus that was nudged and spliced to where it is today. As it is by itself, the vax is just what it was called a cure for the common flu, and it would be harmless to the health of the patient, with the exception of eliminating the flu.

At this time Vonni and Nate had been waiting for the Asgardians 777 computer to finish decoding the fourth files they had. The 777 was making progress. The machine has decoded all but the last file that was written in a foreign language. This language was not known to anyone, or at least on the 777. This computer was well versed in all past and present languages, it was almost as difficult as hieroglyphics. But this language seemed familiar. Seems it is a cross between, Adamic, Cuneiform script, Sumerian, and Akkadian. All three date back long before the Egyptians. The 777 has accessed the encrypted web for additional information on the four different ancient original languages, and will learn and adjust, and in a short time it will learn what the language is. In the meantime, the 777 has produced a brief on the completed files. The Gilgamesh team with Hanna Torres will receive the document at the same time, and a copy will be sent overseas to the Gilgamesh 2 group that Yossele has in place. After they all read and digest the brief they will confer as a team via encrypted satellite transmission and decide what the next plan of attack is.

Chapter 35

The BOJ-25:33 Cure (Two Parts)

Hanna and the team studied the first decoded files and then had the conference call, via encrypted satellite. They discussed the state of affairs that the mission was in and the cure Boj-25:33. They all agreed that the cure was not a world-shattering event, and the disease it cured was virtually unknown. From a layman's point of view, this disease couldn't be detected. The Gilgamesh team and especially Hanna felt they had missed something. This cure as it is, was for sure groundbreaking in the fact that a virus could be used to kill another virus. This new approach would open doors to other studies. However, the Gilgamesh group couldn't understand the importance of the cure and why so much time and revenue was invested. This didn't sit well with them. They knew the answer must be in the next file that the 777 was working on. Tensions were high, mostly because of the lab compounds experimenting on humans. The secret intel they received was that the group, Knights of Noah was involved and that would mean only one thing. That this file on the cure was just the tip of the iceberg. They hoped that the last file that the 777 was working on would shed some light on the first file.

At the same time that the Gilgamesh group had decoded the file for the cure, Dameks team, Fredrich Becker, and Frieda Von Helm had the last and final pieces of the data dump, and they put the final grouping in order. The two sat back and could see the unrestricted data and they seemed happy. Frieda was more into it than Fredrich because she was a Clone scientist, and this file showed so much promise, over and above the cure she could see. Still, she could see that this file was incomplete. Her thought process was why were so many additional viruses worked on and mutated? Even after the initial cure was developed, and Frieda Von Helm was just as suspicious about this whole research as was Hanna Torres. They both believed that there was something missing, and Frieda was going to do the research and find the missing links, as was Hanna.

Frieda didn't have the luxury of the 777 nor the coded files of Meir Alter but she had full access to all of Dameks' lab's computers. She would leave no stone unturned until she got to the bottom of the cure. She expected that there was a part two of this cure and that it was close at hand.

Both Fredrich Becker and Frieda Von Helm informed Damek of the completed file with the cure. He was euphoric and informed his crew of two that the labs would make the cure and at the same time make massive amounts of the Jud-12:6 VAX. This did not go unnoticed by Frieda Von Helm. She silently questioned that order. She wondered why such a large amount of the Jud-12:6 VAX was being produced. She would start her own secret investigation on that.

Damek knew that the cure VAX would take some time to produce and now he wasn't in such a hurry. But the flu VAX Jud-12:6 was a different story that was now a priority, because it was part of the larger plan he had for it. Production started on the two viruses Vaxes and the labs across the world were working on this project non-stop 24-7. Damek estimated, and calculated the amount of the Jud-12:6 vax that was needed and he added an additional 25 percent for incidentals. The amount that was being produced could inoculate the whole world and another 25 percent.

Damek quietly informed his family members of the cure. This took some time because they were scattered all around the world and communication had to be covert. Dameks family although close and in touch with each other in an encrypted way were as a family unknown to the world as being related and that was by design. As the Damek family received the message they were all blissful and could now relax at the thought that the Plague, or scourge that has befallen on their family would end. What the family members didn't know was the scope of the cure and the ultimate price that would have to be paid. That bit of information was withheld by Damek because he didn't want, and wouldn't stand for dissension in the ranks or the family. Damek was the family leader and his decision was law.

The 777 was still working on the last file that had numerous lock boxes, or vaults and this system was proving to be quite a challenge, however, the 777 computer was getting closer to completion of decoding. After the software was done and it learned the system it would redo the complete file as many times as possible to increase the accuracy. The file had so many coded lock boxes that entered into additional lock boxes all with their own individual coding, and then when the files are opened they would need to be decoded. This large file had 7 sub-files and each subfile had three additional lock boxes and they each had three more and that process went on for eleven times resulting in one file having approximately 33 such files times seven and then each had to be decoded, a monumental feat and time-consuming. However the Asgardians 777 was up to the task and was now in the final stages of rewriting the briefing and relearning as it goes for accuracy, however, the 777 has one file that it has not been able to crack and to date has not made any progress in opening it, and the only data the 777 has on this mysterious file is the name and that name is,

Gignesthai -(Greek gignesthai, meaning “to be born”)and the 777 is putting almost all of its resources to work on this sub-file. With each hour the 777 seems to be getting closer to scratching the surface, or making sense of it. The code(ᾳ Ω+,- 1111+ 0,1,1,2,3,5,8,13,21,34,55,89,144,233 #+-%~*) that was on every file was getting worked on, and the 777 was just about ready to crack that code or key to the coding as it is. If the 777 could just open a small crack in the file then the rest would open in a short time. A brief was also uploaded at the same time as the last, stating that this one file was still being worked on. Hanna Torres and Juan were happy about the previous files and they wanted the data and intel on this last secret super encrypted file, They felt with that information they would have the complete picture and what they’re up against.

Unknown to the Gilgamesh team and Dameks team was that the Gignesthai file had two files in it. One was part two of the Cure and the second was of the History of Dameks family. This is written in only one other place, and that’s at Dameks home personal file. Only one other person was ever allowed to view it and that was Meir Alter. This original file or book as it is, was written in original ancient scribe. One that no one has seen for years. Dameks family tree goes back a very long way and this book is so accurate and revealing that the presence of the book outside of Damek's house has never happened.

Damek let Meir read or at least view the book in its entirety, feeling confident that Mier could never figure out what was written. Even though Damek knew that Mier had a photographic memory and total recall he was sure the book was safe and couldn’t be reproduced in any way. The language that this history book was written in was a version of the Canaanite group, a long-forgotten language. Mier Alter was a curious man and would work on the deciphering of the history book. He was so moved by what he found that he felt compelled to write down what he had discovered, in his own code.

What Mier Alter discovered in the the Canaanite book that he was able to memorize from Damek, sent chills down his neck. He knew that Damek was a powerful, and extremely intelligent man who was smarter than Alter, and the deciphering and rewriting of the secret history book gave Mier insight into why Damek was so intelligent. Mier was in awe of his friend Damek. Mier never let Damek know what he had done, if he had, Damek most certainly would have dealt with this breach of his privacy.No matter how good of a friend that Mier was to Damek this information could never be known.

Chapter 36

Vax Part One Of Two

As the two vaxes were being produced, the BOJ-25:33 cure was the first one to come out of the incubators. There was enough of this new secret vax to cure all of Damek's family and then some. Damek was in the process of delivering this miracle cure to the family members, via through the normal vendors that you may find on the corner of an intersection that sells medicine across the world. The vax was in injection form and each of the family members would receive a prescription for the medicine. This would make the shipping of said Vax much easier, and the multitude of family members could take it at their own discretion. When they all had been inoculated they would let Damek know. This process would take some time. This gave Damek the breathing room for the labs to manufacture the massive amount of Jud-12:6, flu vaccine for distribution. Damek would need to get very active in the distribution technique or systems. This was a two-part system for the delivery of the Jud-12:6. Damek knew that the second system would be difficult, but not impossible. He again would need to put all his influence, power, and money into play. He had planned for this very moment in time. But still, the project would be a massive undertaking, and the delivery would need to be so top secret that even the top intel agencies were not aware of the infrastructure that was now in place for this mission.

Yossele Schumacher, was working across Europe and the Middle East theater watching and investigating the labs that had the human testing camps. He made several insider contacts with head administrators, using the same tactics of money, bribery, and when necessary blackmail. He was receiving a lot of information that was similar to the other lab camps. That was that a great many of the human test subjects were dying suddenly and a small percentage of them were not affected. Yossele was doing extensive research on the cause, and with his inside people, he was getting a handle on the exact cause. As he was assembling his research file, Yossele had transmitted what he had so far to the team leader Hanna Torres. She in turn would put it into perspective as only she could do. The deaths of the lab Camp test subjects triggered her thoughts about the Jonestown people temple massacre. Although she knew this was different she felt the same eerie feeling that this was not an accident because the same event seemed to be happening at every known lab camp they had under surveillance. Hanna requested that Yossele get more information and use whatever means were necessary. She wanted to know what killed these people and why. The next question she asked was why did some of the subjects show no signs of getting sick or dying. Hanna wanted the medical files on both the deceased and the survivors. She made it clear that Yossele should make every effort to get this information. It was just that important. Hanna was getting to a point of frustration that she had never been at and she wanted more information. The fact that they had a secret coded file in their midst and still couldn't access it frustrated her. She could see or feel that this whole Cure project was coming to fruition. Hanna didn't like where she thought it was heading. Yossele sent Hanna a coded message that indicated that he was close to getting what she wanted and that it would come in a flash drive. He also informed Hanna that he would share his findings with his agency the Mossad.

Vonni and Nate were still working on the South American camps and working on what they could find. They discovered that the lab camps there were experiencing the same dilemma. These camps were losing a major portion of the test subjects. They were working on getting the reasons why. This information just reinforced the ill feeling that Hanna was getting. The puzzle was looking more and more like a complete picture, one that Hanna could only see.

Several days later Damek received confirmation that every one of his family members had received the vaccination for the cure. This would begin the next phase of his final solution. Damek could see that the next part was close but that the labs that are manufacturing the Jud-12:6 vaccination, had almost completed the daunting task of getting the Jud-12:6, ready for shipment. The time frame was close and the reports were that it would be ready within the next 24-36 hours. With that number in mind, Damek proceeded to put the delivery plan in place. This would take more than 24-36 hours. What Damek wasn't aware of was the fact that the Gilgamesh team was closing in on what the labs were doing. He didn't know that they had the two damming files that could kill his projects. Damek thought he had more time, but the Gilgamesh was relentless and so was Hanna Torres. Her inner radar was on fire and she knew this was getting close to critical mass. Hanna would run the results up the ladder to her superiors and she would have to make a plan for what should be done next. That was almost impossible because Hanna didn't have all the intel. All she had was her theory. That was usually more than enough to make the higher-up move on a mission. But this time the cost for a probable was just too high and the bosses needed concrete data before they would go to the the next Defcon level. However, they would start the process of deterrence and keep it in the wings for now, at the starting gate and ready.

The Jud-12:6 vaccination had started to ship across the world and the amount that was needed was still not at the full capacity. But Damek was getting the product out there and in position for the next phase.

At this time the Asgardians 777 software had made a dent in the last two files and was decoding at a slow pace. the 777 printed out a brief that the file could be completely decoded within the next day or so, and no other information was printed. This new information excited Hanna to no end and she awaited the final copy. The tension was so high in Hanna and her mission group that they all needed some R&R time. They couldn't do anything pending the final decoding of the Gignesthai (Greek gignesthai, meaning "to be born" file). So they as a group and under the close watch of SS agents went to dinner and drinks and talked about anything but shop. The tension level reduced by about fifty percent which was good for the whole mission group.Yossele was given the night off as well and he went to dinner with a lady friend in Europe. Yossele relaxed as much as he could and that wasn't a whole bunch. Because Yossele was always on edge and he preferred it that way, he would relax in his own way, and that would require that this mission was completed. Yossele was the same as Hanna in many ways and could read between the lines. He put together a scenario that most people couldn't fathom, and that's just the Mossad way. This mission in his mind, was super important and his inner thoughts were that if things got out of hand or went sideways, this would not end well. From past experience, Yossele felt that his country Israel may not fare well and he would do whatever he had to for the safety of his people.

The Gignesthai file was decoded and almost fully opened. The 777 software was just redoing the files and would have the results sooner than anticipated. These two files couldn't be in brief form, they would need to be in full PDF format for the team to read. The formatted files were extensive and would take time to read and absorb. From that point, they would make whatever plans were needed. However this would not be completed for about 10-12 hours, and the team could decompress.

Chapter 37

Part Two, Section Two

The Asgardians 777 computer with its unique decoding software, had completed the decoding of the final two files and made a printout for the Gilgamesh team. Before they were able to read it, both Hanna and Juan would need to read it first before the team. Because of national security claims and the way management does things, the two read the first file that the 777 made. They were put in panic mode, and this was foreign to both of them, because they both controlled their emotions. But this file, if true was devastating to the people of the world.

The file went on to explain that there may be a plan to send a seemingly harmless vaccine out to the world that was coined or called the Jud-12:6 vaccination, and according to the file if implemented this vax, was a trigger virus. That means that this simple flu virus would trigger other viruses to come out of dormancy. The virus in question was an ancient virus that was a cross between the Spanish flu that killed 50 million and the virus called Black Death or Bubonic plague. Both of these viruses have left their DNA remnants in the human genome and are dormant, or part of the sequence. The Jud-12:6 vaccine wakes these two viruses up and they become an active mutated strain, that causes the victim to get very tired and then fall into a coma-like state. Then the virus attacks the immune system and the lungs, and the person dies from fluid in the lungs or pneumonia. The mortality rate is near 90 percent and the only ones that survive are the people that have a rare blood type of Rh-null, AB-, B-,

AB+. These individuals are for the most part scattered across the world.

The Jud-12:6 vaccine works in reverse of some other viruses, or the Virophages and some viruses kill each other and negate the threat. This Jud-12:6 vaccine, man made designer virus wakes up specific dormant viruses. That's what happens when an overzealous bored biotech scientist wants to see just how bad, bad can be, and this is their creation. The reason the Jud-12:6 vaccine was developed in the first place was that it would also hunt down and eliminate all remnants of an ancient virus that has been dormant for thousands of years in human DNA. This particular dormant retrovirus is the cause of the Dameks family curse, and per the file, if the remnant of this retrovirus still exists, then the Damek family will get reinfected and their curse will continue. So per the file, this ancient virus and its carrier, the 90 percent of the population need to go away for Damek and his tribe to survive.

Hanna and Juan were aware of the Jud-12:6 vaccine being distributed across the Globe and the two decided that was going to be their top priority. Time was of the essence and they would need to jump into action to prevent the VAX from getting distributed. The thought was that once this Pandora Box was opened this new designer virus would linger and stay in the air and eventually infect the whole population. The mutant virus would not affect Dameks family because they have already been given their personal vaccine the BOJ-25:33, and this would delay or eliminate the effects of the Jud-12:6 vaccine on them until they had their complete immunity established. That may take a short time, because the family has a secret that only they know. Once the BOJ-25:33 cure manifests itself, and the family goes through its secret ritual will they be safe That timeframe is rapidly approaching.

Hanna Torres took her finding up the ladder and presented her case. Hers and Juan's response to the crises, was quite simple it was to seize, capture, and apprehend all shipments of the Jud-12:6 vaccine. More importantly, go in and take control of the labs and manufacturing plants. And last but not least, destroy all records of this dreaded man-made virus. What they couldn't do was find out who Damek was. But they now have records of the recipient of the vaccine, and that was a start, or so they thought. Damek always had an evacuation plan for his family, one that he has used many times for a small segment of his tribe. Damek was confident that he had everything in place as plan B to relocate and change the identities of all involved. However, the family would need to go through the phase before the reconstitution and he was sure that wasn't a problem.

The powers above Hanna Torres received the brief and her plan to stop the execution of billions of people. They accepted the plan as was presented but this would have to be kicked up the ladder and additional high-ranking military and political people would need to get involved. These high-ranking people would have to bring together the world's leaders, and they would have to do it in a way that was top secret. This absolutely should not get out to the public, and so the President of the U.S. was informed.She jumped into action and assembled her own team to look at and evaluate the Hanna plan. President Janis Howley would contact all allies, including their close one Israel. The president was aware that the Israeli government and the Mossad were already up to speed and President Howley spoke directly with the Prime minister of Israel. They all agreed on the confiscation plan and the destruction and seizure of said records. The President made calls across the world and sent copies of the files and received complete support. this would need to be a worldwide effort and one that was covert. Especially from the prying eyes of the media, at least for the time being, and that in itself was a monumental task.

The world leader united in a way that they would send their military out to confiscate the Vaccine. But first, they stormed the labs and the manufacturing plants to find out where the Jud-12:6 vaccine was shipped. They found that thousands of containers of the VAX were unaccounted for. This was a big problem, and the search was on. As the labs were taken over one by one the records were searched for the whereabouts of the missing shipment. They searched one after the other and couldn't find where they were, until an I.T. Professional discovered where these shipments went. He discovered they were sent across the world and they were not in the form of injectable syringes and needles but in another form that was more lethal in its own right. This form of medication distribution was entirely different than what is the norm. The thousands of missing containers were in the form of a gas and can be administered through another means that has been said to have been done before, but has never been proven. The method in which these missing containers would be used, was what was coined years ago as contrails/chemtrails. It was originally thought up in the 1960s when jet planes were seeding the atmosphere for weather. Then thoughts were for biological agents. The idea was that a high-flying mega jet could get into the many jet streams and disburse the Jud-12:6 vax. These jet streams would carry the agent across the globe and infect the remaining population that couldn't or wouldn't take the Jud-12:6 vax. This vaccine, virus would take its course and cause mass and catastrophic die-off of over 90 percent of the human race. The race to locate the whereabouts of these canisters was of the highest priority. However, means were taken by Damek to hide the travel and shipment routes, and time was not on their side, but they would continue the search.

Hanna Torres and Juan were sitting with their team and they discussed the situation. They all agreed that the chemtrail was just as serious as the actual injections, and that the location of the canisters was more important than just about anything. Hanna decided to let her Gilgamesh team work on locating the canisters and she pulled Juan aside. They decided to read the second decoded file to see if it had any clues that might help them with their mission. Hanna and Juan went back to her study and started to read the second file and this was not in brief form. The two wanted to read the un-briefed version because they didn't want to leave anything to chance or miss a single line that was in the original version. They informed the Gilgamesh group that they would be indisposed for a time, and to continue with their work on locating or resolving the missing Jud-12:6 vax canisters. Hanna and Juan gave instructions that they should put every and all options on the table and even if it's so far out there that it was out of the realm of logic they wanted all options. With this, the very talented group would work into the night, and Hanna and Juan had their work cut out for them as well. Again time was their enemy and every minute counted.

Chapter 38

The Gignesthai File Of Dameks Memoirs

Damek wrote that his first memory was when he woke up, and opened his eyes. He could see the crystal blue skies, and smell the flowers, other vegetation, and fruit growing. Damek's first thoughts as they were, was that he had absolutely no memory of his past. He was lying in a field of thick green moss, that was so soft and lush that he didn't want to leave it. His age was approximately 16 years old and he couldn't speak any language or walk at all. All he had were his instincts to survive. The area that he woke in was a mild jungle setting. It was full of fruit trees and small animals and the temperature was in the 80s. Damek had to crawl around on his hands and knees before he acquired the ability to walk on two feet which took less than a week. Damek's thought process was just to survive, he had no others. As time went on he would learn to walk better and pick fruit, take care of himself, and bathe in the warm streams. Because Damek had no memory he had no languages. Any thoughts were fleeting and instinctive, and that would change in a short time. He was extremely intelligent and learned quickly. He would hunt small animals for food because he couldn't survive on fruit and he wasn't a vegan. Damek would wander around this jungle area for a period of time exploring and learning and in time developed his own language that he would use as thought. Still, he didn't know how to speak. That would come in due time. When the spoken language came it was shrill and full of grunts and noises that didn't sound the same that was spoken in Dameks mind and he worked on that. However, since he didn't have anyone to talk to that process would take a long time. Damek learned to make his shelter and by hit and miss, he became quite a builder. The shelters would keep out the rain and winds when they came, and that was rare, but he liked the feeling of a roof over his head. After several years of his personal growth and his maturing Damek would find out why he was in the beautiful Jungle paradise. This revelation would come suddenly and since Damek had never seen danger he wasn't frightened or scared.The discloser was presented to him, and with his superior intellect, he would accept the divulgence of his existence. This is when his creator God would first speak to Damek. The words were spoken telepathlogy and Damek could see GOD but the image was out of phase or blurred. That was because no human can lay eyes on GOD, Exodus 33:20. God said you cannot see my face, for man shall not see me and live,— and that was why the image was out of phase. The Creator GOD said his creation needed a name and he called him Adam and the name Damek is actually Adam in Slavic. GOD said that ADAM needed a helper or mate and at that time he put Damek into a deep sleep and while he was sleeping GOD took one of Adam's ribs and created Eve, and Adam said "This is now bone of my bones and flesh of my flesh; She shall be called 'woman; for she was taken out of man. Adam and his wife Eve were both naked and they felt no shame,(The pictures of Adam and Eve) are incorrect as they show both having navels, and since neither were born they could not have one.

Some would ask how a brother and sister or someone that have the same DNA could marry and produce children and not have defects and the answer is that both Adam and Eve have the exact DNA and genes and since they do, their offspring would not be subject to recessive traits or defects. Their offspring would have the same good genes to reproduce without issue.

As time went on Adam and Eve reproduced and had many, many children.Eve had multiple twins, and the clan would grow and grow.

Both Adam and Eve had perfect genes and they had the ability to fend off any and all disease. They also had instant regeneration, they would heal in hours which takes days or weeks to repair the body when it is injured.

Their life span was off the charts because of the perfect gene pool they had. They would age just like all humans did and their aging would cease at about the twenty-year mark. From that point, they would age differently. They age in a normal way, for about fifty years and at that time a unique type of metamorphosis would take place and this molting as it is. The subjects would fall into a deep sleep for about 24 hours. At that time the Molting would start and finish and the old body of seventy-plus years would again regenerate, or molt back to its original form or age of twenty. It would shed the skin and old cells, and renew itself to the twenty-year-old body. Because of the perfect DNA and genes that Damek and his offspring have they could and would regenerate as many times as needed. If severely injured their bodies would take time to regenerate, and in some instances look as if they had passed away. If the body was hurt badly enough, such as a chest injury or heart damage, the brain and other organs would go into deep hibernation and wait for the repairs to be completed. This may take hours. If the person was on a battlefield they would heal and come back as good as new, and the scarring would go away soon after the injury. If an eye was lost the subject would have to wait until they molted again to form a new eye or appendage.

The land that Damek, (Adam and Eve) were created was called the Garden of Eden. It was a beautiful place, and more, this large body of land was secure and isolated from the rest of the world in a way that it was a large island. Somewhere between the size of Greenland. But larger than Australia and located crossing the Equator between the Continents of Africa, and the Western Hemisphere. This land mass was later called by a myth name, Atlantis. This island as it was, had fast-moving ocean currents running up one side and down the other causing the island to be almost unapproachable, and inaccessible by almost all sailing vessels. Unless the ship was designed to navigate the ultra-high currents and tides and the surrounding coral reefs. The people of Atlantis had been on earth for a millennium, and knew how to make the ships necessary to enter and leave the island.

The island Atlantis, (Garden of Eden) that Adam and Eve were created on had been home for his family and now clan. The population had grown and would grow to a number of 144,000, all with the same DNA and gene pool and all with the same life span. That was, for lack of a better term, eternal. On this famed island, God put many many resources for the inhabitants. The Creator also put two trees that were called the Tree of Life, and the Tree of Knowledge of Good and Evil. The Tree of Life gave the gift of Immortality and the tree of Knowledge of Good and Evil presented a choice between obedience and disobedience. Per the Book of Genesis, eating from the latter forbidden tree resulted in a separation from God. But this was not true, per Damek, the separation from his Creator was not from the tree but from what his clan did and what was forbidden by Damek and God.

Dameks' family grew in population to the grand number of 144,000 (the chosen). At that point, his people stopped having offspring, which was caused by what is referred to as clone fading, or replicative fading. That occurs when the DNA sequence begins to mutate and a genetic drift begins, and the end results are the ending of reproduction. The only solution is to introduce DNA from a non-mutated (un-faded) sequenced individual. Damek was fine with the amount of family members in his tribe, and so were all of the population. Introducing new DNA wasn't an issue or option.

Atlantis and her people the Adamic were around for a millennium before humans came on the scene. Humans began or were caused by the Adamics themselves. Because in their travels around in their very sophisticated ships, and going to Africa and exploring other countries, these Atlanteans would collect many of the monkeys that were more intelligent than others. They would train them to do menial jobs that the Atlanteans didn't want to do. The fatal Sin, that caused the Adamics to be evicted out of the Garden of Eden or Atlantis was the interbreeding with this monkey race.God the Creator and Adam forbid this. However the tribal leaders still did it, and the Monkey people would produce what is now called Homo sapiens. This new species would eventually evolve into what is called humans that are present today. This new species looks remarkably like the original Adamics or Atlanteans. When the Creator saw what his people had done, he condemned the whole tribe, and expelled them from the Garden of Eden. At that time the island of Atlantis would begin to sink. This event would take some time and gave the group time to relocate. Because they, as travelers with mighty ships decided to relocate the family, this would require years of trips to the new home. They decided to go to the north, because at the time the climate was warmer than it is now. The new location was Greenland and Ice Land, and the hunting was good and fishing was as well.

The new location was perfect and Adam is the Patriarch of the family and as such he would sit on what is now considered a throne. Adam would surround himself with many of his closest family, of first sons and daughters who were the oldest but still in their regenerative youth.Adam's first sons were big in stature and he wanted his closest, strongest near. They would run the family like a government with Adam being the ultimate leader, and a myth would begin and spread throughout history. Adam would no longer be called Adam. He was now referred to as ODIN, or Allfather (father of all gods). He was the chief deity of the Aesir family of gods that reside in Asgard, and known for his great wisdom and knowledge. The Norse Mythology would be written and had more truth than fiction.

The Norse Gods in time decided to branch the family out to nine realms and different parts of the world. Adam would still be the Patriarch. He allowed this and gave very specific rules that as his family moved to other parts of the world that were now populated with the advanced monkey homo sapiens population called humans, and because these humans were inferior Adam instructed his family to refrain from mating with the humans and only mate with the other family members. That meant that a prince, could only marry a princess from another kingdom that was from the original family. Because they all had the same DNA, or their genes were not polluted by the human monkey race, and because they would Molt back to a younger age they could rule the land forever. However, that order was not followed to the letter, and the family leaders in other countries would succumb to temptation and mate with humans. This mating would be the cause of the curse and family disease that has plagued the Damek family for thousands of years. The plague that is killing his family is that they are slowly losing their ability to molt or regenerate back to the age of twenty. Every molting leaves them older and the end is getting dangerously near where they will just get old like the monkey people and die.

The breeding with the Monkey people is the original Sin that caused Adam and Eve and his family to lose the rights to the Garden of Eden.

The breeding with the Monkey people and mixing of DNA and genes with this inferior race would be the ultimate cause of the GAIN OF FUNCTION mutation and cross between the two species of a virus. Because this gain of function could never have occurred if the gene pool wasn't polluted or degraded. The Adamic DNA could not stop or fight the mutated virus that was developed because the Adamic immune system didn't see it as a threat. Because it was a gain of function, it now had parts of its DNA and genes and could hide and be undetected by their killer immune system. This was the single virus that Damek was looking for a cure. He had it in his hands and his family was now vaccinated, so they were safe for the short term. However, his family could be reinfected with a mutant form of the same virus and that meant that the carriers of the said virus would need to go away before the virus in question mutated and the cure became ineffective.

Damek would do whatever he had to for the protection of his family. He had the plan in motion and thought that nothing could stop it.

The BOJ-25:33 manufactured virus that was administered to Dameks' family would not only kill the intrusive ancient virus that his family had been infected with at the DNA level, but the BOJ-25:33 would also completely remove the DNA fragments of this virus from their blood. They would once again be as before. The original perfect creations of God, with the perfect DNA and genes. If all things went as planned the Adamic clan would continue to thrive and live as immortals, that the world still has no records of or idea that this large population of people are among them.

The number of family members that started at 144,000 from the beginning does not have that full amount anymore. Due to deaths due to the destruction of their bodies. With that kind of damage even their regenerative abilities and immune system the injured family members could not and did not survive. The total number left has been depleted by about ten percent or 14,000. The Adamic family knew they weren't indestructible, and for years have taken measures to avoid any area or situation that would put them in jeopardy. In essence, they became more cautious. Some because the world had become somewhat safer and mostly because they were in a position of authority and wealth that they could avoid dangerous encounters. The Adamic group has not lost any family members in well over 2000 years and the progression of getting old and molting back to the age of twenty again and again was not even noticed by anyone. The person that molted was pronounced dead and they always had an Heir that would show up just after the molting and fake funeral, and the legacy would continue and continue.

Chapter 39

Chem-Trails In The Sky

The Gilgamesh team searched for the canisters of the BOJ-25:33 agent and found that it may be impossible to locate the hundreds of them. They could not find the distribution systems or all the jets that would emit this deadly agent into the atmosphere, and the jet stream for worldwide disbursement of the vaccine/virus. They might be able to find all of them if they had the time, but that was quickly running out. Both Hanna and Juan had to come up with another contingency plan to neutralize the threat. The two would round table with their Gilgamesh team. The only thought or counter to what was just about to happen was that the Gilgamesh team needed to speak with Damek, or at least communicate with him and try to make a deal. The whole team thought this was a lost cause, because they knew what was at stake with the Adamic family, but they had no alternative. The survival of the world was at hand. After researching the documents, they found they could reach out through an obscure email account that was virtually untraceable, because the account would change venue so rapidly and access was limited to just Damek and whoever he let in.

The Gilgamesh team sent out a plea for help or at least a communication with Damek. In it, they stated that they were aware of what was about to unfold and that they had the identities of almost all remaining Adamic family members. There would be a massive search for them and a worldwide warning about what Damek was up to. This may or may not derail his plan, but they put this request out there for Damek to read and hoped for a response. At the same time, the Gilgamesh team was putting in motion a defense for the virus planes that would need to be airborne to administer the agent. This plan would be to destroy the Jet Planes that have the canisters on them. However, just knocking the planes out of the air would not be enough, because the agent would not be damaged and the exposure and distribution would still be present. Just not on the grand scale of injecting the agent into the jet stream as a chemtrail. But the agent would still be out there and it would take months, maybe years for it to travel across the globe. At that time the original ancient virus may recover and re-infect Dameks family. The Gilgamesh group came up with a system that they believed would be more than effective in taking out the agent. They had to convince the U.S. government that this may be the only way for survival. The plan would be to use a little-known weapon called a Thermite Magnesium missile bomb. One that was made for better or worse as some might say by the U.S. and was very large. This particular weapon at full strength would take out almost a half square mile with temperatures reaching in excess of 4,000-4,500 degrees. This revised weapon was top secret and for the most part, banned from use in a war-like theater. This would most surely destroy the agent and the threat. However, every one of the canisters would need to be located and destroyed preferably on the ground. The team was frantically looking for the virus jets and canisters. They waited for a response from the e-mail that was sent out.

Damek received the cryptic email and he was not thrilled with what he read. Damek was reasonably sure that this group could not interfere with the ultimate plan, but again he left nothing to chance. So Damek reluctantly responded with only one word—WHAT?— and the team was extremely happy to have made contact. All the while the 777 computer was still working on the last file and going over the accuracy and rewriting the files trying to achieve the high 90 percent rate in accuracy. As the 777 was doing well, it was finding several parts of the secret encryption file to have additional information. Some were interesting and important to the success of the group's mission and the possible end to this showdown. The 777 was within a couple of hours of completion of the final brief and it was a game changer.

Damek would have his canisters airborne soon and these jets were positioned across the world. They were just waiting for the go-ahead to commence the atmosphere seeding with the Chem-trails. Damek was watching and waiting for the best weather pattern, and he watched the jet stream predictions. Damek wanted the vaccine/virus to reach the population in a controlled manner and all at the same time so the virus infection would take place in unison across the globe. Damek saw that the weather pattern was getting extremely close to the drop-time and he thought he had everything in place, until he received the e-mail from the Gilgamesh team. That stunned him and caught him off guard, and that didn't sit well with him. Damek had a plan B in his arsenal, and in the plan, he had a multitude of additional vaccine canisters hidden away for what he called a spoilsport response. If the first wave of Chem-trails went south or was destroyed, Damek had these canisters hidden well, and he could unleash them at a later date if needed.

The Gilgamesh team located the jets that had the canisters loaded on them, and was in the process of confiscating all of them on the ground. But that would take several governments all cooperating at the same time. The seizure of the planes needed to be timed perfectly so all were taken within minutes of each other. However, Damek was aware of this movement and he accelerated the timeframe, and would have the jets in the air soon. As Damek caught wind of the order to go in and take the aircrafts and the payload, he launched them all at or about the same time and they would reach the altitude of the jet-streams. These high winds reach speeds of more than 275 mph and the streams heights vary four to eight miles. These streams are in both the northern and southern hemispheres. The distribution, when done correctly would blanket the planet with the virus. The amount of jet planes to accomplish this feat would be twenty. Ten for the north and ten for the south. These aircrafts would reach their destinations in about two hours. The Gilgamesh group saw the launch of the twenty jets and were alarmed at the quickness and deliberate move that Damek just made when they thought they had opened a communication door. When these planes were in the air the Gilgamesh group leaders rushed to the higher ups and presented the case and the need to accelerate the timeline and plan for the destruction of the now airborne jets. The people that have the authority to order the destruction of these commercial type planes would do just that and they sent the order up the chain. Since the military was already on call for this emergency, it took less than ten minutes to get the countermeasures up and ready to deal with the threat. The many fighter jets in that air pursuing the now airborne jetliners were equipped with the improved secret weapon called the Thermite Magnesium missiles and since there were twenty aircraft with canisters loaded the military sent up well over 80 intercept attack jets. They left nothing to chance. Each fighter jet had two of the Thermite Magnesium missiles loaded under their wings and they were locked and loaded and now airborne themselves, and on the hunt. Damek knew when these fighter jets were launched and he gave the order to disperse the cargo at the earliest time even though it wasn't the optimum time. The Chem-trails would take several hours or more for full dispersion, and once started and the virus was let loose there was no turning back. The new mutant killer virus would take the world by storm and the carnage would be on the stage of Biblical proportions. The race was on and Damek had an Ace up his sleeve, or a plan B, in the event that the chem-trails jet planes were destroyed.

As the virus-laden jet planes were airborne and trying to get to the desired altitude, the order was already given to destroy them ASAP. The attack fighter jets searched the sky for the virus-laden jetliners and knew where they were and the heading. But the intercept was a time-related element. Some because of the speed of the virus jets and their range, and the limited range of the chase jets. All in all the airborne virus jets were just 20 across the globe and the attack planes would need to refuel in-air to chase them down. The attack planes started their air-to-air mission. As these fighter jets located the virus-laden jets, they would get into position to release their payload. The pilots had their special visors positioned on their helmets that would darken automatically when the super bright thermite bomb ignited, so they wouldn't be blinded. Just after the rockets/missiles are deployed the attack fighter jets would need to begin a hard dive away from the point of ignition, and the ride for the pilots would be rough. The Thermite bomb would suck all oxygen from the area.A combination of the explosion and then as the air was consumed, a vacuum would occur and cause such turbulence in the sky that the fighter jets would get tossed around quite a bit. The men and women flying these jets would have their hands full just trying to keep the plane level and under control. It turned out some of the fighter jets were destroyed as well as the pilots.

The Thermite Magnesium missiles began destroying the virus-laden jetliners one by one and the missiles were very effective. They completely destroyed the virus. As the search and destruction of said jets went on, Damek watched and monitored the whole situation from his computer screen. He had access to the the top-secret data, and he was furious. As he watched the destruction he just nodded his head and decided to instigate plan B. But Damek would make contact with the person who engineered this whole campaign, and that was Hanna Torres. He sent an e-mail-type instant message to her that simply stated that she had won the battle but not the war and that he would initiate part B in the next couple of hours. That there was no stopping the next move, and that the carnage would just take longer than the first plan. Hanna received the E/message that was virtually untraceable and she went pale because she did not know this Plan B. Because of this she couldn't formulate a defense. Hanna responded and said she would concede to his authority and she requested that Damek give her 6 hours to respond.Damek refused, however, he stated that the implementation of plan B would take about six hours and he would contact Hanna just before V-Day-(Virus Day).Hanna gave her thanks and started what may be her last meeting with the Gilgamesh team. As they all assembled, either by computer screen or in person they would debate what to do next. At that time the Asgardians 777 computer had completed the decoding of all the files and made a brief for them to read. The very last page showed an interesting twist that no one saw coming. As they all read the brief it brought to light a possible solution to the crisis and that gave them hope. They would read the brief again and again. Hanna decided to take the finding/solution up the ladder and see if a deal could be made with Damek. She went to her superiors and presented her case and her plan and they were fully aware of the time limitations. They agreed to do whatever it would take to make this happen. With the final approval of the higher-ups, she went back to her group and developed the response, and how to sweeten the deal so Damek would take it and spare the world from extinction.

Hanna messaged Damek that she needed to speak to him ASAP. He did not respond immediately, and as they waited for a response they hashed over the proposal. They all agreed that this was the only option they had, and hoped that Damek would agree to their terms.

Damek, after another hour, responded to their idea. He wasn't sure why he responded to the monkey people, but he did and what he heard was, and if this was true he now had a plan C. He said to Hanna that he would get back to her within the hour, he would need to review the offer and the data she has from the Asgardians 777 computer and confer with his technicians to verify if what Hanna states is true or possible and with that he severed the connection.

They all waited for a response, from Damek, and the Gilgamesh group sat in silence for quite some time before Vonnni broke it. She said they should work on another plan in the event the Damek rejected the offer. Both Vonni and Hanna knew that working as a team would help the mood and give them a purpose for right now. The total extinction of the human race as we know it, is at hand. Just sitting by was not their M/O.So they would debate the next possible move and the distraction was just what the team needed.Hanna Torres had a special team working on finding the position of the last communication, and that was futile at best, but they tried. Every jetliner with the original mixture of the virus was destroyed and no trace of the killer virus survived. If the plan B Damek had in place was implemented then the hidden canister of the dreaded virus would be opened and the killer would be released. The transmission of the virus would take time for it to travel across the world and every step of the way would leave a trail of death. The results would be the same but take weeks or more to travel and infect everyone. The time for the deaths would not be in days as would the Chem-trails dispersion and that would be unfortunate. But Damek wasn't a psychopath and he wanted a way out. Because he became fond of the monkey people and in the back of his mind he knew that most of them (monkey people) had some of Dameks very own DNA and that was just like a distant relative. That's hard to just eliminate so Damek was in a quagmire and his immediate family came first and the distant relatives by DNA would be considered only after.

Damek would confer with his scientist and they all worked feverishly on the data that he received and the results of their findings, although preliminary would give Damek the information he needed. They all waited, Dameks scientists didn't know what lay in the balance or what the results were. They went on facts and did not know what was about to unfold.The data file was finally completely gone over and they agreed that the data was good and that the cure to the cure was, in fact, real as written by Meir Alter. He was the only monkey person that Damek ever trusted. And with the news, Damek would need to make a response plan or guarantee from the powers that be. He would put his demand out to the Gilgamesh group and they would have to sell it to the government leaders. Damek put the words on paper and was still working on the response when the one-hour mark came up. Damek would at that time send an e-message to the Gilgamesh group, and state he likes what he's read so far and has given them another hour reprieve, and he continued with his paper demands.

The plan B that the Gilgamesh group sent was that Meir Alter had found a cure for the plague that had invaded the Adamic people and the cure was that another man-made virus would attack and eliminate the virus that Dameks people had. This new attack virus would not only destroy the original ancient virus but at the same time it would remove all strands of the plague's DNA from Dameks tribe and at the same time give the Adamic people back their natural immunity from the virus ever entering their systems again. Damek only gave this data any Creedence because Meir Alter had written it.

Damek returned the e-message with his demands and it went like this.

1-The world must never know of him or his people.

2-All data on their research would be destroyed.

3-The world would never know the real history of mankind.

4-Damek would put the remaining canisters in deep freeze to keep the killer mutant virus, in the event that parts 1-3 of this contract were not followed.

5-they have ne hour to respond.

As Hanna read the terms she was nodding her head in agreement and presented it to her Gilgamesh group. They read it and almost all agreed with the terms, except for Vonni and Nate. They wanted to add an addendum to the agreement, and that was that all the secret labs be closed down and that the test subjects at the labs be released unharmed.They also wanted all records of the dark web human trafficking and the people involved. They wanted the harvesting of human organs stopped. This was a huge demand but both Vonni and Nate were hopeful the demand or addendum would be honored. Damek received the response and read it and thought that the whole human race was balanced on this demand. He shook his head and thought that maybe there was hope for the monkey people. He agreed and would send the information to them, but he had to first get his secret labs producing the cure for the cure and that would take a short time. Damek had everything in place to gene splice and mutate the viruses and the deal was struck. A stand-down order was given on both ends and Damek ordered the killer canister put in deep freeze. The captive people of the hidden labs were being released in an orderly manner.

Hanna Torres was and is a stubborn overzealous researcher and she in part agreed to the terms. But in the back of her mind, she couldn't let it go, not so much to alter the agreement but because she wanted to find Damek and see him in person. She wanted to see someone who was touched by God our creator. She now had an obsession and the search would have to be so quiet and under the radar so that the agreement was not rescinded.

Damek in time revealed the data and people involved with human trafficking, and human organ harvesting. In that data, it was discovered that some countries had secret facilities that would harvest healthy organs from trafficked people and then dispose of the remains as they would sell the unused parts to other labs for research. Almost none of the donor's body parts were wasted. This would lead to a crackdown on all black market organs and make selling them a capital offense. In addition, the second part of human trafficking is the slave trade which has been said to be higher than at any time in history. Many countries ship their people out to other countries for work and the mother countries receive compensation. These people who are sent out are used and abused in unimaginable ways, doing whatever the host country or in many cases cartels wanted the slave people to do. That included hazardous conditions and or prostitution, and in many cases, the slave people were used as test subjects in experiments. To the powers that control the populations of these countries, people are a cheap commodity that they grow in their backyard and have no other thoughts about them, just a means to their wealth.

The deal was made and completed but the Mexican standoff was that the data that Hanna Torres and her group had would be buried and never see the light of day.Damek would in turn hide the deep frozen virus canister and the world would survive. So would the Adamic Tribe and no one would be the wiser. So the data files were destroyed with the exception of a master file that was mislabeled and buried in the archive, and Damek would make a fail-safe system on the canisters. If the power was lost and the battery backup went down the canisters had a self-destruct mechanism that would start a cremation sequence of the canisters and their contents.

Both Damek and Hanna Torres saw the deal as the best they could get, and Hanna in the back of her mind vowed to find Damek and meet him, her only wish was to see and touch someone that has spoken with God the Creator and get some insight, to the beginning.Damek would watch Hanna from afar and monitor what she was up to, he had the resources to do just that and the wealth.

Epilogue

The world was saved and so were tens of thousands of trafficked people and many of the ring leaders were brought to justice. However, none of the fully vested people involved in the trade were found or implicated,(Money talks and protects). Hanna would go back to her regular routine, and from time to time do a dark web search on the Adamic people and Damek. She would do it in a way that was not detectable. Just small peeks at different data. She could and would assemble this data into a readable file as only Hanna could do. She would work on this personal mission until she found what she wanted. The danger was high, not only for Hanna but for the human race, so she had to go slow.

Damek would also watch what Hanna was doing and her progress. From his point of view, the minor research and data were benign at best. Damek wasn't aware of the unique way that Hanna's mind worked and that she could assemble a file from snippets of information. However, Damek would keep track and cross that bridge if and when a new threat came up. Damek Hava, the first man on earth, the name Damek, because boasting an intriguing mythological feel, Damek is a masculine name rooted in the Biblical Adam. Slavic in origin, Damek embraces the original Hebrew name's meaning of the red earth as its own. His last name Hava, means Eve according to the book of Genesis, Adam's wife, the first woman to be created—(Eve. , Chava, Chavah, or Hava and Damek liked to play with words as did Meir Alter, so the name Damek Hava actually means Adam and Eve.

The code that was listed on the bottom of almost every page of Meir's files—ɑ Ω+,- 1111+(0,1,1,2,3,5,8,13,21,34,55,89,144,233)#+-%~*was broken down by the computer 777 and it found that the Alpha Omega (ɑ Ω) signs mean the beginning and the end in the greek alphabet. The code at the bottom of the page would change and sometimes have a - instead of a + and that would trigger the reader to relate or read from the end to the beginning of the page for clarity. This would go on throughout the files, almost unnoticed. The next part of the code is 1111. This is the Angel number, and much has been written about this. The next part is of course the Fibonacci sequence or the golden ratio of 1.618 and the sequence shows up across the universe in almost everything and Meir Alter knew this sequence and added it to the code to confuse a computer from breaking the code.

Vonni and Nate went back to their villa in South America and they started to see thousands of missing children and adults who were trafficked return to the country. That would make the whole mission a success for these two.

The file BOJ-25:33 was actually in code as it was transversed and should be read as Job 33:25 the Scripture and its meaning —His flesh shall be young like a child's, he shall return to the days of his youth:::let his flesh be restored and become fresher than in youth—That is what the cure BOJ-25:33 would do for the Adamic people that have started to age because of the plague they have from an ancient Virus.

The Adamic tribe has been with us since the beginning and they have influenced the evolution of the monkey people with the infusion of their perfect DNA. As the Adamic people left the Garden of Eden or what has been referred to as Atlantis, they migrated to Greenland and Iceland at that time the weather was warmer and the continent was not covered in ice. These ancient people were super intelligent, and as the myth goes, this tribe was called the Norse Gods because of their ability to regenerate and repair their bodies if injured. The fact that they were immortal, these traits would make these Adamic people look like Gods in the eyes of the monkey people. As time went on for them they would spread out and move across Europe and other continents and become rulers like Caesar. Some would look at them as Gods. The only Roman Emperor who proclaimed himself as a God was Suetonius Caligula and he was assassinated just like Cesar. In any event, these rulers knew that they had to marry within their own tribe and would accept princesses from the other 9 realms of the Adamic people across Europe and the intermarriage would keep the perfect DNA they had. However, at times they would succumb to temptation and mate with the monkey people and that would be the cause of their plague. The cross-mating would excel the monkey people in their evolutionary path to where it is today, and without this perfect DNA flowing through their veins, the evolution and sheer advancement of the inferior race would not occur, and be what it is today.

The Mexican standoff was that both sides held a trump card, and if the contract that was made was not respected, then one side of the deal would be devastated. Again Damek had no intentions of hurting the monkey people, but would if pushed into a corner. So Hanna Torres should be very careful in her research, because Damek was always watching or at least one of his henchmen was, and he is Immortal.

www.ingramcontent.com/pod-product-compliance
Lightning Source LLC
LaVergne TN
LVHW010548160826
845677LV00013B/3051

* 9 7 9 8 8 9 4 0 6 1 8 3 2 *